You Can't Cheat Death

by

Peggy Doviak

A Magnolia Hill Mystery

Cover Art by *Najla Mahis*

The Wild Rose Press, Inc.
PO Box 708
Adams Basin, NY 14410-0708
Visit us at www.thewildrosepress.com

Publishing History
First Edition, 2024
Trade Paperback ISBN 978-1-5092-5735-5
Digital ISBN 978-1-5092-5736-2

A Magnolia Hill Mystery
Published in the United States of America

Dedication

For my great-grandmother, who started my storytelling, and my aunt, Margaret Beggs, who helps it continue.

Acknowledgments

The publication of You Can't Cheat Death is a dream come true! I have loved mysteries since I started reading The Bobbsey Twins and Nancy Drew. I devoured my mom's old books along with new ones bought for me by my grandfather while he was on business trips.

Thank you to my tremendous editor, Ally Robertson, for all your hard work and support. Thanks, also, to The Wild Rose Press (TWRP) for believing in my dream.

Thank you to my publicist, Nancy Berland, for playing a critical role in my writing career. Look where we've gone! Thank you, John Charles of The Poisoned Pen Bookstore, for suggesting recipes for financial success at the end of the book instead of the cooking recipes I was considering. What a great idea! Additional thanks to my friends in the Tornado Alley Chapter of Sisters in Crime and Route 66 Sisters in Crime critique group. Your belief in me buoyed my confidence when I wondered if I could pivot from nonfiction to fiction.

Thank you to my family and friends for so much encouragement. Naming people always leads to the fear of excluding others! To all my writer friends, I'm immensely grateful for your support. Thanks to Sheila Roberts for sharing your social media platforms and Marie Bostwick for sharing your blog. Thank you, Tee O'Fallon, for help with plotting and titles over espresso martinis. Thank you, Val Clarizio, for making me feel so welcome. Thank you, Marcia Preston, for reassurance every time I said, "I know I should know this, but..."

Thank you to fellow TWRP mystery author Dianne McCartney for assistance with details of the publishing process. Special thanks to Jo Carol Jones, for letting me be part of the Book Lovers Con family and helping me make so many new writer friends!

Thank you, Jennene. You know which character you inspired! Thank you, Patty, for listening to endless revisions. Thank you to my family, both by blood and by marriage. I love you all very much!

Thank you to my great-grandmother, who when I was very young, played make-believe, listened to my stories for hours, and read my early writing efforts with great seriousness. Much love to my aunt Margaret Beggs, my superfan, who is up for anything and feeds me when my schedule is crazy. Finally, thank you to my amazingly supportive husband, Richard Doviak, who now looks out for me from beyond.

Chapter One

The hot Oklahoma sun beat on Jillian's arms, and she leaned against her shovel. Her horse, Agatha, lived in a world far removed from Jillian's financial planning job. Named for Agatha Christie, one of Jillian's favorite mystery writers, the sorrel mare had no interest in cash flow statements, retirement projections, or market returns. Some grain, hay, and a peppermint treat or two kept her happy. At the ranch where Agatha lived, Jillian's stress level usually dropped by the minute. But not today.

She had finished cleaning her horse's run when she saw an altercation brewing between two residents. "Mister," she called out. "Mister," she yelled louder, "leave her alone. Can't you see she doesn't want you around?"

Jillian could tell by the girl's glare that she didn't like the attention when she moved away and tried to ignore the mouthy taunting.

"Seriously, stop bothering her," she yelled again. His flashing brown eyes dared her to do something about it. Jillian gazed down for a minute, weighing her options. She was alone, and if she tried to intervene, she would need help because of his size.

A loud yelp interrupted her dilemma.

"Agatha! Bad horse. I know he's annoying, but don't bite Mister!"

Agatha pinned her ears against her head, and Mister, the black-and-white paint horse in the adjacent run, realized he'd harassed her too much. He backed away, no longer trying to chew on her gray mane. Agatha charged the fence in response to his retreat and tried to bite Mister again. But he had moved well beyond her reach.

Jillian laughed at both of them. "Come on, Agatha. Leave him alone. I've put down some hay." She stepped back so the angry horse could see the newly cut green Bermuda that smelled like summer.

Jillian liked cleaning the run, preferring the dust and muck buckets to gyms where everyone admired themselves in mirrors. She also hated touching all that sweaty gym equipment. At least she knew the source of everything she shoveled.

Half a dozen different bird calls broke the silence. Jillian's eyes scanned the grassy horse turnouts separated by white metal fencing. She found the source of the music at the top of a power pole beyond the gravel road. A joyful mockingbird imitated blue jays, crows, bobwhites, and several birds Jillian didn't recognize.

Tired of her war with Mister, Agatha finally trotted over to Jillian, put her red head down, and sighed. "Good girl! You'd better play nicer with the other horses, or we can't ride in the parade."

The 4th of July was just around the corner. They had ridden in parades before, and all had gone well. Still, Jillian didn't want to go flying down the route, leaving a trail of red, white, and blur.

Jillian set down her shovel and grabbed her grooming bag. She brushed Agatha's mane, still damp from Mister's mouth, and took inventory of her chores.

She had dumped and refilled water tubs, cleaned the run, and tossed hay in the aluminum feed trough. Certain she was done, she kissed Agatha's head.

"I'll see you tomorrow, pretty girl. I've got to go make a phone call to Nancy." Agatha either nodded in response or rubbed a fly.

Jillian's client, Nancy Hampton, had worked with her forever, and her email said she had something important to discuss. Her tone sounded odd, like she was upset about something, but Jillian couldn't imagine what. They talked regularly and had carefully structured Nancy's finances and accounts to help her meet her goals.

Jillian put the brush back in her orange canvas grooming bag and gave a final rub to the star on Agatha's forehead. "I don't know. Wish me luck. I think I'll need it." Agatha nodded again and sighed, seeming to agree with Jillian's concern.

The eight-hundred-acre ranch sat just off a quiet road, but Jillian always stopped and checked both ways before she pulled out. Before she could turn, a yellow Porsche convertible flew by her from the right. Her ex-boyfriend, Stan Savage, owned the only yellow sports car in Magnolia Hill, but Stan wasn't driving. Instead, a middle-aged woman with frizzy brown hair peered over the steering wheel, a grim expression on her face despite the cheerful rock-country music blaring from the radio.

Stan's assistant, Betty Dingle, was tearing down the road, but why would Betty be driving Stan's car? Because of their history, Jillian dodged Stan since his return to Magnolia Hill. She glanced back at the fast-disappearing Porsche, shook her head, turned left, and headed home.

Peggy Doviak

After a quick shower and change from barn shorts to tailored beige slacks and a brown sleeveless blouse, Jillian turned into a financial planner again. She combed out her damp, long blonde hair and put it back in a ponytail. A little eyeshadow echoed the green in her eyes. Then she laughed—Nancy wouldn't care what she wore from the other side of the phone.

Once she had added earrings and brown flats, she located Edgar, her cat. He lay snoring, passed out on her couch, air conditioning allowing him to curl in a small black ball. He lay there quietly, but a shiny eye watched everything she did. She carefully closed her front door, making sure he didn't make a last-minute dash for freedom.

She climbed into her pearl-black F150 pickup and headed toward her office. Even though she had only been home about an hour, air-conditioned seats helped cut the searing heat that had already built up in the cab.

During an Oklahoma summer, shade, not distance, defined good parking places. Jillian got lucky and parked directly under a tree in front of her large office windows that looked out on the turn-of-the-century buildings of downtown Magnolia Hill.

She loved growing up here so much that she even attended a nearby university. Distant big cities held no allure. After graduation, she moved back and ultimately opened a financial planning firm in the two-story brick section of town that resembled a Western movie set.

Today, though, her office seemed cold and foreboding while she got ready to place the call to Nancy. No doubt, the dazzling June day made the inside artificial light seem dim, but most of the darkness came from her sense of dread. Even the painting of Agatha

4

wearing sunglasses didn't cheer her up. Jillian sat down, took a deep breath, and dialed the phone.

Nancy's voice shook, and her words sounded a million miles away. Jillian's chill increased, and her hands began to sweat.

"So sorry… I've loved working with you… Stan just promised such good returns… Three members of my bridge club use him… He's made them so much money…"

It took a second for the meaning of Nancy's words to penetrate Jillian's mind. Her client was leaving her for Stan Savage, owner of the yellow Porsche and Savage Financial, whose corny motto, "Let Savage Slay Your Financial Dragons," had made Jillian laugh until that minute.

Nancy's words brought her back. "I hope you don't take this personally."

Jillian pulled herself together, glad to be talking on the phone, and she wiped a stray tear from her eye. She summoned her best cheery voice. "Of course, I don't, Nancy."

She hoped the tone hid her heartbreak. "Please don't hesitate to call if I can help you in the future." After Jillian choked out a few more pleasantries, she hung up.

Hot tears stung her eyes, while she tried to make sense of Nancy's words. How could one of her favorite clients dump her? The older woman's words sounded frighteningly similar to what her grandmother had said all those years ago. Her experiences being scammed had shaped the course of Jillian's career, and now she was angry and suspicious of Stan's promises.

To anyone who didn't know him well, Stan Savage had a good reputation in Magnolia Hill, graduating with honors from high school. Those close to him, however, knew his good grades were often the result of his getting others, usually Jillian, to do his work for him. As he grew more manipulative, he lost some of his charm, and those who cared about him the most, including Jillian, became disillusioned. By the time he announced he wanted to leave the town for a bigger stage after their senior year in high school, Jillian had cried for a while but soon threw herself into college classes and activities. She didn't miss him much after that.

But after many years away, Stan had apparently missed Magnolia Hill because six months ago, he returned to town and opened a financial firm. He'd rapidly made the rounds to everyone who knew him when he left, and he'd developed a remarkable investing reputation, a small-town boy who made it big. Several people had told Jillian about Stan's ability to make money; however, Jillian knew that unless Stan had been a very late bloomer, he didn't have the mental capacity for Warren Buffett's talent. What was going on?

Chapter Two

Jillian leaned back in her chair and closed her eyes. She remembered when Nancy started working with her right after she had opened her practice. Over the last dozen years, Jillian helped her client when her husband unexpectedly died while mowing his lawn, when her daughter divorced an abusive husband, and when her granddaughter needed money for college.

She wanted the best for Nancy's future and rejoiced when she could play a role in her success. Like the broker had treated her grandmother, Jillian believed Stan didn't care about the older woman. Instead, he only valued the best things he could buy from the money she paid him.

When she opened her eyes, she sighed at the stack of files on her desk. Her assistant, Katherine, always took off the two weeks before the 4th, so the planner had more paperwork than usual. She'd file it later. Now, she needed to talk to Allie. After a quick text exchange, they agreed to meet at Bits, Bytes, and Brews in fifteen minutes.

Allie Kowalski and Jillian had been best friends for thirty years, inseparable since they met on the playground in first grade. Now a painter, Allie never arrived anywhere without a smudge on her skin or clothes. Jillian walked into the noisy, fragrant coffee shop, scanning the tables for her buddy. She saw Police

Officers Gayle Johnson and Jeff Stone at the corner table. Gayle glanced over while Jeff turned away. Beside them, Will Anderson huddled over his laptop, typing away on a story for the local newspaper, *The Magnolia Daily*. Jillian sighed with relief when she spotted Allie in another corner of the café. She could happily go the rest of her life without telling Will hello.

Her friend always stood out with her short, platinum hair and paint-splattered shirt. Allie's project of the day seemed to focus on something green—dark green, light green, and lime flecks appeared brighter than the other colorful splotches on her yellow T-shirt and overall shorts. Converse tennis shoes finished her outfit.

Jillian shook her head. If she went out in public wearing paint-covered clothes, she would appear ridiculous. But Allie's free spirit had a personality brighter than a neon palette.

Allie waved, but her high-wattage grin dimmed when she saw Jillian's red eyes. "Oh, sweetie, what's wrong?"

"I lost a client today. I can't believe it!" Jillian's eyes betrayed her and filled with tears again.

Allie got up from the table and put an arm around her shoulders. "I'll get us coffee, and you can tell me about it. You want a 'Summer Special'?"

Jillian nodded and watched her friend walk toward the shiny chrome counter. She glanced around aimlessly, trying not to cry in the middle of the coffeehouse. Fortunately, Will focused only on his computer, and Gayle and Jeff seemed involved in a serious conversation. Beside Allie, the chalkboard on the counter announced the coffee special. The PB&J contained peanut butter-infused coffee with strawberry or grape syrup. Beside the blackboard stood a metal shelf filled with baked goods to go, but today, they held no appeal.

Soon, Allie returned with two enormous iced coffees piled high with whipped cream. She set one in front of Jillian and said, "Okay, spill the tea, but not your coffee." Jillian knew her friend wanted to cheer her up, but she was too upset.

Before she had the opportunity to tell her story, Kandace O'Connor rolled up to them in her custom wheelchair. Kandace had opened Bits, Bytes, and Brews a few years earlier and turned a tedious restaurant into a bustling, trendy coffeehouse and internet bar. She lived upstairs in the mixed-use building accessible by an antique elevator.

Kandace learned the traits of hard work and perseverance in high school when a hit-and-run driver left her in a wheelchair. From that day forward, the determined young woman constantly fought to get stronger and live a normal life. Her ability to create a thriving coffeehouse surprised no one.

She smiled at them both, but it faded when she saw Jillian's red eyes and Allie's grim expression. "What's wrong?"

Jillian poured out the story of Nancy and her anger at Stan Savage to both of her friends. When Jillian said Stan's name, Allie's eyes narrowed. "That no-good June bug. Stan has been nothing but bad news since high school."

"Yes, I know. I should always listen to you." In spite of herself, Jillian laughed at Allie's colorful description comparing Stan to the goofy insects that flipped on their backs and scooted across patios on summer nights. Allie avoided profanity because her grandmother hated cussing, often leaving her with creative language choices.

Allie's blonde head bobbed back and forth. "At least you got rid of him eventually. Too bad he's back in town."

Kandace appeared lost in memories, sitting quietly until she leaned forward. "I've hated Stan for years. I've always believed he was the driver who hit me that night."

"What? Why?" Jillian and Allie asked together.

"Even though it was dark and I was badly injured, I'm sure I saw a red sports car leaving the scene after it hit me. I tried to tell the police, but they didn't listen."

"Stan always had a sports car," Jillian remembered. "Back in high school, he drove a red Corvette. I remember his driving habits changing. When he was sixteen, he drove like a maniac, but he slowed down, I don't know, maybe in our junior year." She paused. "About the time of your accident, Kandace. I never put it together until now. Why didn't you tell us what happened?"

"Because nobody listened to me." Her eyes filled with tears she should have shed years earlier.

"It probably didn't help that Stan's father ran the city council," Allie grumbled.

"No," agreed Kandace, wiping her face fiercely with the back of her hand. "Some attorneys talked to me in the hospital a couple of times, but then they dropped it. Even my insurance company couldn't prove anything."

"I can't believe you had to go through that while you needed to heal," Jillian said.

Kandace shrugged and motioned around the room. "I try not to be bitter and focus on what I've managed to achieve. Still, I'll never trust him, and I'm sorry he hurt you and your client, Jillian."

"I hadn't thought much about his coming back," Jillian admitted. "I never thought he was a threat. Pretty stupid, I guess." She stabbed the whipped cream with her stir stick, mixing it into the coffee.

"No, your clients should appreciate what you do for them," Kandace protested.

"Tell that to Nancy's bridge group. They convinced her to leave me for Stan."

"Then they don't know what they're talking about. I wonder if they understand why you opened your business in the first place. Do you tell your clients why you went into finance?" Allie asked.

Jillian shook her head.

"You should. It's a great story!"

"I know, but I hate to make my grandmother seem stupid when she wasn't." She viciously stirred her coffee again.

"But you changed your life for her," Allie pressed.

"I did," the planner admitted. "I just couldn't believe what that broker did to her. Imagine putting an older woman into risky stocks just because she said she wanted to make money." Even today, the story infuriated her.

"All I'm saying is that she was lucky you wanted to step in."

"I didn't know much about the stock market then, but I knew what he had done was a bad decision."

"You found your passion, and you saved her," Allie insisted.

Jillian again marveled at the loyalty of her friend. Despite her distress over Kandace's revelation and Stan's recent behavior, she appreciated her friend's encouragement.

"Gram was worth saving. I think that's why I'm so angry about Nancy."

"You work like crazy to keep your clients safe, and you know Stan's not going to do that."

"No, he's not. I wonder what he's telling everyone."

"I bet he's schmoozing them, telling them they're smart, he likes their shoes, and their hairstyle makes them look young. Then he convinces them to buy investments where he makes a lot of money. We need a spy in that bridge group." Allie smiled slyly. "My *Babcia* plays bridge. I wonder if she's heard anything."

Allie loved using the ethnic name for her Polish grandmother, Penny Krol. Even though Penny remained proud of her heritage, she was no one's meek old lady, laying waste to common stereotypes of vulnerability. Instead, Allie's spunky grandmother knew everyone in town. She would have heard about all the details of Stan and any line he told her friends.

Allie texted her grandmother, who always kept her high-end cell phone handy. No surprise, Allie's phone pinged back almost immediately. "*Babcia* says if you're not busy, come over after we finish our coffee."

"Good deal! Let me know what you discover." Kandace brushed her shoulder-length brown hair back from her face and tossed it behind her purple T-shirt.

"Oh, we will," Jillian promised.

"And ladies, try to stay out of trouble." She laughed and waved to her friends as they headed for the exit.

As Jillian opened the door, the fierce Oklahoma sun temporarily blinded her, and she ran full force into someone.

"Jillian, what's the rush?"

She recognized the voice before his features became clear. "Stan?" The last person Jillian wanted to run into, literally or not. In spite of the heat, her chill from earlier in the office returned.

"Yes, it's me." The way he said it, he sounded like a pompous superhero wannabe. "Here I come to save the day!"

Anger choked Jillian's throat. She needed to get out of there, but Stan seemed determined to talk.

"So I'm working with one of your old clients now. No hard feelings, right, hon?" Stan stood beside a woman Jillian didn't recognize—a difficult feat in this small town. When he started goading, the glamorous blonde took his arm to lead him away like she had done it before.

Jillian silently gagged when she saw that even their clothing seemed coordinated. Stan oozed high-end country club—pink polo shirt, khakis, and loafers. The woman wore a Madras plaid dress accented with excruciatingly high-heeled pink sandals. Jillian marveled at how much hair spray she must use to keep her platinum waves in place in the Oklahoma wind. The brief diversion helped her capture her voice.

"I won't discuss clients with you."

"Nothing personal, you know, hon. Just business."

His infuriating arrogance reminded her of the day they broke up. Back then, he left no doubt that he thought he would achieve more than she could. Old and new anger charged her voice. "I don't know what decade you think we live in, but I'm not your 'hon.' "

Stan's chuckle made Jillian fists clench as her voice rose. "I also don't know how you're showing clients impossible returns, but I'll figure it out, and I'll bring you down."

She felt all the eyes of Kandace's patrons, and sensing an audience, Stan became indignant.

"Hey, hon," he exaggerated the last word, "I just have a better system than you do, so people would rather work with me. I make them more money." He flashed an angry look around the coffeehouse, and the customers quickly returned their gazes to iced mochas and lattes.

The blonde actively tugged on his arm, but he paid no attention. Jillian could barely see from her anger, and she ignored Allie's frantic gesturing for them to go.

"Drop dead, Stan," she screamed, storming to her truck parked near his yellow Porsche. He said something else in response, but her slamming door cut off his words.

Jillian put the truck in drive, cut the wheel hard, and barely missed Stan's fender. The late afternoon sun glared in her eyes, so she grabbed her sunglasses and pressed the accelerator harder. Someone needed to teach that man a lesson.

Chapter Three

When Jillian pulled up to Penny's house, Allie's tangerine Prius occupied the middle of the driveway. How could a car that small fill two places? She laughed despite her anger and parallel parked on the street in front.

Penny lived in a 1950s red brick home with white wood trim, a porch in front, and a mail slot. Her flower beds bloomed with pink, orange, and yellow zinnias. Bunches of daisies dotted fresh red cedar mulch. Even though the wooden front door stood open behind the glass storm door, Jillian rang the bell. Allie unlocked the latch and let her in.

Penny already had lemonade and freshly baked *kolaczki* pastries on a tray in the living room. Her parents had emigrated from Poland, and she often made recipes passed down for generations.

The gardens brightened the living room through large windows, and the interior decor continued the theme with vivid floral drapes and couch pillows. Allie had inherited her grandmother's love of color.

Penny came up and hugged Jillian. She had worn the same cologne forever, and the young woman found herself enveloped both by loving arms and the fragrance of tea roses. "Jilly, child, what's going on? Allie told me you wanted to talk."

"Thanks, Penny. I need a smart second opinion, and Mom and Dad are studying stone circles in England."

"At Stonehenge?" Allie asked, glancing up from a sketch pad she kept at her grandmother's.

"No, the British Isles have many ancient circles. They're in Northern England right now."

Jillian's dad, an archeology professor of some renown, taught at the local university unless he was conducting research in the field at a dig. Recently, her parents had begun to visit some of the world's most impressive sites—Machu Picchu, Egypt, Mexico—so many remarkable locations and compelling artifacts. She jokingly called her dad "Indiana Jones."

Their frequent absence led her to consult Penny when something troubled her, and her best friend's grandmother enjoyed the role of confidant. Jillian figured if Penny had heard anything about Stan's scheme, she might offer details and advice.

The older woman poured lemonade and passed the tray of *kolackzis* while Jillian collected herself. Despite her distress, the Danish-like pastries made her happy. She selected a cherry one and bit into the flaky crust, savoring the combination of fruit filling and powdered sugar icing. After a sip of the cold lemonade, she summarized what had happened. Penny cut her off at Stan's name.

"Of Savage Financial?" she asked. Jillian nodded, and the older woman's eyes narrowed like Allie's had earlier. "I warned you years ago about him."

"Just like your granddaughter." Jillian laughed.

"I haven't changed my mind," Penny said. "Of course, half the women in my bridge group think he walks on water. Me, I'm not so sure."

Jillian leaned forward in her pink Queen Anne chair. "Why?"

"He's called me a couple of times trying to get me to transfer my accounts over to him. He says he can select the stocks, bonds, and funds in a way I would like. But there's something about what he tells me, or more specifically, what he doesn't."

Jillian looked at her, hoping she would continue. No fear. Penny talked without encouragement.

"He never mentions risk," she explained. "Instead, he keeps saying that he can help me earn more money on my investments. When I ask him how, he laughs at me, saying his methods are complicated and that I wouldn't understand them. Bless his heart." Her final Southern epithet didn't care a bit about Stan's heart. She stopped and stared directly at Jillian, simultaneously lowering her head and glancing over her glasses.

Her face made Allie howl with laughter, but it froze Jillian's ability to swallow, and she snorted the lemonade up her nose. Through choking and chuckling, she asked, "He doesn't know anything about you, does he?"

Penny had done her own investing for years. Sometimes, she called Jillian with a question about Federal Reserve actions or a change to the tax code, but she never asked what she should buy or sell.

"He thinks I'm a stupid widow—a doddering old fool who needs a savior."

"Like he's some kind of a superhero," Jillian said, and Penny nodded.

"Exactly. He acts like everybody's savior, but I don't trust him."

"Do you think Stan's promising high returns to your friends?"

"Think it? Child, I know it. Even more strange—he's delivering. At least, that's what they tell me. Every single week, before we sit down to play, they remind me that I should let Stan manage my money. One week, my friend, Marge, brought her investment statements to show me. She even made money when the market went down a couple of months ago!" Penny drained her glass of lemonade and reached to fill it again.

She pointed the pitcher toward Jillian, but after a large coffee and a lemonade, Jillian had to shake her head no. "How odd. Could you see the investments?"

"No, they weren't on the statement, at least not on the pages she brought. Marge said he claimed to have a 'proprietary system.' "

"Yeah, I bet." Jillian scowled.

As Penny thought about what her friends had told her, she glanced away, and no one said anything. In the quiet of the room, the wall clock ticked incessantly. Suddenly, she made eye contact again with Jillian.

"One weird thing just happened. Marge needed some money from her account. Stan promised to get it for her, but a couple of weeks later, she still didn't have it. When she called again, he apologized and said he'd get the check right out to her. He sent the money this week."

Jillian surprised herself by coming to his defense. "Well, sometimes a client request slips your mind."

"I know, but Marge said Stan sounded nervous. He started hemming and hawing when she called back asking for the money again."

Alarm bells rang in Jillian's head. "Do you know how much money Marge asked Stan to send?"

"She needed about a third of her investment

portfolio sold and sent to her bank account. She wanted to finish paying off her house and some other bills before she finally retires for the last time," Penny explained.

"Marge just loves to work. She substitutes three days a week at the grade school since she retired, but she's finally ready to stop teaching altogether. After Stan sent the money, she made her final house payment."

Jillian had mixed feelings about mortgages but understood Marge's desire to pay off her debt. "I'm sure your friend will like not making house payments during retirement," Jillian said. "You know it doesn't matter why she needed it. Stan should have sent her the money the first time she asked for it." Penny nodded in agreement.

Jillian finished her lemonade as the warning bells rang louder. Marge needed money, and Nancy's account could pay for Marge's request. Had the timing been a coincidence?

"Penny, do you think Marge would show you her statement from Stan again?"

"I don't know why she wouldn't. She's still trying to convince me to work with him, even after she had trouble getting her funds."

"Stan casts quite a spell. I don't suppose she'd let me see it, too."

"I'll ask," Penny said.

If Jillian's suspicions were correct, Stan didn't have a stellar trading plan. Instead, he kept his clients happy in a less honest way. But she needed more information before she said anything.

Chapter Four

The day after her confrontation with Stan, Jillian spent an entire meeting trying to convince her client, Dave, not to put all his savings in cryptocurrency. Even if someone eventually created a reasonable alternative to the US dollar, Jillian believed his enthusiasm and desires were over the top. Crypto had a short track record, widely varying fans, and too many recent trading scandals. An hour and a half into the meeting, Dave finally seemed convinced.

As she finished her summary notes after he left, her phone pinged. Penny's message said Marge would discuss Stan's strategies. Allie's grandmother asked if she could pick up Jillian in half an hour, and the planner texted back with a thumbs-up.

Soon, they zipped down the streets in Penny's white Lexus convertible, the top down despite the temperature. The hot wind made talking difficult, and Jillian breathed a sigh of relief when they finally pulled up in front of a white clapboard house with a giant oak tree in the yard. While she tried to smooth her blonde hair into something presentable, she glanced over at Penny, whose short white layers had settled into contemporary spikes.

Allie's grandmother rang the doorbell, and a frail woman wearing jean capris, a white T-shirt, and slippers shuffled to the door.

Penny gave Marge a warm embrace. "Thanks for making time for us, friend. Meet Jillian."

Jillian extended her hand, and Marge returned the handshake, her cold hand showing protruding, blue veins. "It's nice to meet you, Marge."

Marge opened the door farther. "Please come in out of the heat!" They stepped inside, and Jillian could hear a window unit air conditioner running like mad. The spotless home smelled vaguely of bacon, cologne, and mothballs, and it appeared darker and older than Penny's riot of colors.

Marge led them to her family room and flipped off the game show channel on the television. She waved toward a white velvet couch with swirls of dark green. "Have a seat. Do you mind cats?" She motioned to a white Persian lounging on the footstool. On cue, the giant cat raised his head and yawned.

"No, I love them," Jillian said. "What's his name?"

"Romeo. He's my buddy. Can I get you two anything to drink? Penny, do you want some tea or something stronger?"

"No, I'm fine. Thanks for agreeing to talk to Jillian."

"I'll discuss Stan, but I want to make clear that he's treated me very well."

Jillian gently raised her hand. "I believe you. I'm just curious about his strategy. Can I see the statements he gives you?"

Marge appeared concerned. "Yes, but you won't show them to anyone else, will you?"

"You can trust me."

"I know, dear. Penny's told me stories about you for years. You and Allie have a knack for getting into trouble."

Jillian laughed, wondering what Allie had told Penny. "I will categorically deny anything too bad."

"You can't deny the piña colada story."

The memory made Jillian giggle. "What a mess! We didn't know you couldn't make them in a food processor. When the liquid started leaking, the whole kitchen got sticky! We had to wipe up every inch while we tried to corral Allie's dog, Boomer, and keep him out of the rum."

Marge and Penny laughed. Jillian believed both women were born knowing how to use a food processor.

Finally, Penny asked, "Did you at least get a piña colada?"

"No, we didn't have a blender! We just stirred up rum and pineapple juice while Boomer sniffed every inch of the kitchen and licked up several spots we missed."

"My land, dear, of course, you can see my statement." Marge took off her glasses and wiped her eyes with a tissue she already held. "And I trust you. No one who lied would admit not knowing how to use a food processor."

Jillian gave her a slightly ashamed smile. "Do you want to email them to me?"

"I don't do much of that, but I can let you borrow the paper copies. Just bring them back to me in the next couple of days."

"No worries. I'll take pictures of the pages with my phone now."

Marge walked to the other room, and Romeo bounded after her. Penny winked. While Jillian snapped pictures, the two friends murmured about the disastrous haircut a mutual acquaintance had just received from the new salon in town. They seemed to think she deserved it after cheating on her regular beautician. After Jillian had the images, she handed the papers back to Marge.

"Thanks so much." She gave the older woman a quick hug.

"No problem, dear. If you find anything interesting, let me know. I think Stan's actions will impress you. If you borrow any of his ideas, I'll never tell." She held her fingers to her lips conspiratorially.

"Thanks again! I'll keep you in the loop," Jillian promised.

Marge hugged Penny, and the threesome walked into the Oklahoma heat. This time, Penny relented and left the top up while they drove back to Jillian's office.

****

On her way home that evening, Jillian grabbed Chinese takeout. She pulled out of the parking lot and was surprised to see a news helicopter fly overhead toward the river. She watched it for a second and then turned her truck toward home.

Edgar met Jillian at the door while she struggled to juggle her takeout bags, drink, and briefcase. "Hey, kitty! Did you have a good day?" A cheerful meow suggested his day went well.

Named after Edgar Allan Poe, the kitten appeared one day out at the barn. He wouldn't let Jillian out of his sight while she finished her chores. After a few questions to friends, it appeared the tiny black ball of floof didn't have a home. She took him back to her place that night, and after a few months, he couldn't remember his barn cat career.

He followed Jillian to the kitchen, and she plopped the bags of food on the counter and her briefcase on the

Navajo-print chair at the wooden kitchen table. Although Jillian enjoyed Penny's floral prints, she preferred the warmth of southwest colors and patterns. In the distance, she heard a helicopter again while she unpacked dinner.

Surrounded by carryout containers of fragrant hot and sour soup, crab Rangoon, and Shantung steak, she began reviewing Marge's document. Jillian had never seen anything like the statement from Savage Financial. As she reread the data, Edgar jumped up beside her. She broke off a piece of crab Rangoon and gave it to him.

"Edgar, Stan's report makes me nervous. It only shows a chart suggesting Marge makes money every single month." Edgar meowed in agreement or, possibly, in a plea for another bite. She absentmindedly petted him while she kept reading. "It also doesn't list what she owns, and it doesn't have any fine print. This statement smells like rotten crab." Edgar wrinkled his nose with concern. He hated rotten crab.

Jillian dialed Allie, and she answered the phone on the first ring. "What's up?"

"I'm glad Penny keeps stalling on Stan. I've been studying one of the statements, and most of the information is missing."

"What do you mean 'missing'?"

Jillian slipped off her simple black heels and put her bare feet on another chair's red and turquoise upholstery. "The statement's only two pages long with a giant chart taking half the first page, and it doesn't have any required sections like holdings, transactions, and fine print."

"You know I don't know anything about investing or statements, Ms. Financial Planner," Allie laughed. "Translate that into English."

"I won't bore you with technical details, so I'll give you the short version." Jillian took a deep breath before she continued. She didn't want to panic everyone without reason. "I think Stan might be a thief. When the market went up, so did Stan's investments. But his investments kept going up even when the market went down."

"Fish sticks, that sounds just wrong," Allie agreed. "How did he do it?"

"Hang on a second. I need to get Edgar off the table." Hearing the word "fish," Edgar made his move to finish off the last of the crab, and Jillian put him on the floor with another couple of bites.

"Little thief," she accused, and Edgar glared up indignantly. "Allie, do you remember the big case about the financial fraud guy?"

"The guy on the Netflix show running a fraud?"

"That's right. He convinced investors to open accounts, but rather than investing their money, he spent it."

"How did he get away with that?" Allie sounded incredulous.

"He made them feel exclusive, and he showed them great returns. People don't question success. The system broke down if an existing client needed money. Since he had already spent it, he had to get a new client. Then he would pay the old client with the new client's money. The con worked until too many people wanted to get their money at the same time."

"Wow, how awful. And you think Stan's doing the same thing?"

"I'm afraid he might be. I'll call Penny tomorrow." She checked her kitchen clock with its antique brown horse in the middle. "I hate to bother her this late. The news comes on in ten minutes."

"What will you do next?" her friend asked.

"I don't know. I don't want to accuse Stan of anything until I have proof, and then I'll go to the regulators and the police."

"If you're right, do you think his clients can get their money back?"

"These cons don't usually end that way, but I hope so. I'll talk to you tomorrow."

After she hung up, Jillian ate her now-cold Chinese food mindlessly. Had Stan earned his showy yellow Porsche through hard work, or had Penny's bridge club financed it? The thought made her sick.

She pushed her plate away and flipped on the television to watch the evening news. A breathless, grim reporter told the story of a horrible accident in Magnolia Hill. The shot of his face switched to a video of the scene, and Jillian caught her breath as a yellow Porsche emerged out of the river. The reporter announced tragically that the driver was dead.

Chapter Five

Jillian stared at the television. The video shifted to a group of Magnolia Hill police officers, including Gayle and Jeff, studying the road where Stan left the pavement. She knew that section of highway well. Oklahoma has a reputation for endless plains but also has some rugged terrain. The location of the accident had a steep drop-off that required a sharp right turn if you were driving down the hill. If you missed it, you could tumble over a cliff deeper than anything else in the area. A riverbed and multiple railroad tracks filled the bottom of the ravine. The reporter continued to explain that police on the scene believed speed played a role in the tragedy.

The helicopters Jillian heard during dinner hurried local reporters to the scene in time to catch the shot of the tow truck raising the car out of the water. By any standards, the image was gruesome. The mangled yellow metal, caved and dented, barely resembled a car, and the missing cloth top had either sheared off or crushed into the back seat. Jillian's stomach churned at the thought of Stan's last moments. What a terrible way to die!

Her ringing cell phone broke through the television reporter and made her jump. Allie's picture popped up on her caller ID. "Are you watching the news?" her friend asked.

"I just can't believe it."

"Well, I can. Stan probably got distracted by his phone and missed the curve. Sheesh."

"Remember I said just today that back in high school, I used to drive faster than he did? I teased him about it all the time. Of course, he might have changed…"

Allie started to offer another retort, but her voice cut out. After a pause, she said, "That's *Babcia*. I've gotta take this."

Alone again in her living room, Jillian sat on her couch, staring at the TV. The news had cut to a commercial, and she muted it. A memory of high school Stan flashed through her mind, his arm casually draped around her shoulder while they walked to class. Even though he had flaws back then, his easy grin and laughing eyes differed greatly from the man at the coffee shop. An unexpected wave of emotion brought prickling tears, and her stomach roiled again.

The Stan from yesterday had lived hard. His high school smile had twisted into a sneer, and the laughing eyes of his youth now darted narrowly back and forth. That arrogant man was the one who died. Jillian shook her head in disbelief. It had to be an accident, and Stan had lost control. Right?

Edgar jumped up on the couch beside her, stretched out, and put his head on her lap. She reached down mindlessly to pet his ears, and he purred with contentment. Finally, he seemed satisfied with his crab snack.

"Edgar, what do you think?" He meowed softly and licked her hand.

She shook her head and turned off the television because the news had moved on to discussing the weather. She dumped the last of her Chinese food and its carryout containers in the trash. Completely worn out, she headed for her bedroom. Edgar followed along, jumping on her serape-print bedspread with a small thump. She changed into a pink tank top and plaid sleep shorts and crawled between the cool sheets. For a long time, her eyes felt frozen open as the scene of the accident played and replayed on her ceiling. She tried to read a new cozy mystery from one of her favorite authors but couldn't focus on the story. Finally, she closed her eyes and tried to sleep, but images of the crushed yellow Porsche haunted her dreams.

After a restless night, Jillian jolted awake with daylight. Just for a second, her mind felt normal. Then Stan's death flooded back in. She wondered again how it had happened. Even though Stan drove a sports car, she believed he only owned it for a status symbol. Of course, people change. Maybe now, he drove like a maniac.

She unwrapped herself from the sheets she had twisted around herself while she slept and crawled out of bed while Edgar rolled over and closed his eyes with a sigh. Jillian staggered to the coffeepot, measured the fragrant grounds, and wondered how or if she should proceed in looking into Stan's death. Her entering the kitchen motivated Edgar to get out of bed, and his meow reminded Jillian that her next action had better involve his breakfast. She dished up his wet food and remained lost in thought. How could she learn more about Stan's financial firm after his accident and death?

She believed he wouldn't leave incriminating papers at his office. He would keep them with him to preserve their privacy. If the police had found Stan's files at the accident scene, she knew Officer Jeff Stone would ignore any plea she gave to see them. But maybe the police missed something. It would be a long shot, but perhaps if she could locate Stan's car, she might find something to answer her questions.

Chapter Six

As Jillian stepped through a quick shower, she wondered where the police would take a car involved in a fatality wreck. She tossed on denim walking shorts and a T-shirt she scored at a financial convention. Then she threw her hair into a messy ponytail and wandered back to the kitchen. The coffee had finished brewing, so she poured the steaming dark liquid into a silver travel mug and did a quick Google search about accident procedures. The results suggested that after a serious wreck, authorities would impound the vehicle at the police station or a garage. Since Magnolia Hill had a small police facility with only a few parking places, Jillian assumed Stan's Porsche had been taken to a garage.

Several car repair places offered services, but most were national chains. Young employees wearing matching polo shirts would come and go at the beginning and end of each semester. Jillian suspected the police would want to use a place with more discretion and stability. She knew where they would trust the integrity of the wrecked Porsche—Grady's Garage. She grabbed her purse and flip-flops, petting Edgar one last time before she left. She wanted to see Stan's car before someone moved it.

She sat down in her truck, but before she started the

engine, her cell rang. She glanced down and saw *The Magnolia Daily* on her caller ID. "Oh no," she groaned to herself.

She pressed the green button and said, "Hello," not offering her name or any other information.

"Hello, Jillian?" The voice came through her truck speakers.

"Yes."

"This is Will Anderson with *The Magnolia Daily*. Do you have a minute?"

Not for Will, Jillian thought, wishing she hadn't answered the phone. But the upbringing by her mom, dad, and Penny kept her civil. "I have one minute," she said with a soft accent on the word "one."

If Will noticed, he ignored it. "Great," he enthused. "I'm writing a piece on Stan Savage. I wondered if you had any insight since, I guess, y'all ran in the same circles."

Jillian rolled her eyes. Were those words an appropriate way to begin this conversation? He could at least pretend to be sorry. The entire town knew she and Stan had dated in high school. Of course, Will spent all his time racing hot rods back then. Jillian believed Will seemed likelier to fly down a hill and miss a turn than Stan ever did. Back then, Will flew through everything, hurting anyone who got in his path. Unfortunately, after all those years, he still seemed as self-absorbed.

"I don't think I can help you," she answered stiffly. "I had almost no contact with Stan after he came back to town. He kept in his circle, and I stayed in mine."

"Until it overlapped in the coffee shop?" Jillian heard the laughter in his voice, and she gripped the steering wheel tighter. How dare he talk to her like that?

"I don't know what you're talking about."

"Sure, you do," came Will's lighthearted response. "You threatened to kill him."

Jillian said nothing, and when Will spoke again, his voice suddenly sounded serious. "Of course, I know you didn't kill him. I just thought you might know something interesting I could use in my story." He paused, giving her a chance to respond. When she didn't, he continued, "Sorry. I shouldn't have made fun. You doing okay?"

Did he mean related to Stan's death, or was he just concerned about her? She didn't know or care. "I'm fine," she said flatly.

"Good." He stopped again like he expected her to say something, and when she remained silent, he gave up. "Okay, then, I won't bother you. If you think of anything, let me know. You know where to find me." She heard the click of the phone as he hung up.

Not likely to happen, she thought and turned into the driveway of Grady's Garage.

Jillian knew Grady was the best mechanic in Magnolia Hill. His garage was just an old, rusty metal building with a corrugated roof set slightly off the road. But Grady was honest, talented, and fair. He had diagnosed several issues with her last truck, explaining the problem using words she understood and charging a reasonable amount for the repairs. She believed that if the mechanic had examined Stan's car, he would recognize sabotage.

She only saw Grady's legs behind a pickup when she pulled up in front of the garage. He raised his head from the hood of a Chevy, rubbed off any dirt on his pants, and came over.

He extended his newly wiped, slender hand. "Jillian,

I'm so sorry about what happened to Stan."

See, he had much better manners than Will, even though he didn't know her well. She struggled against another unexpected wave of emotion. "Thank you. We barely saw each other since he returned, but it's still a shock."

"I can imagine." Grady nodded sympathetically. "Stan owned a beautiful car that oughta been completely trustworthy. It doesn't drive itself, though." He offered a small smile, revealing worn teeth that showed their age, and he put the wrench in his pocket. Grady wore blue denim overalls every day to work. Somehow, along with his long-sleeved white shirt with the sleeves rolled up, he kept them remarkably clean, given the dirty nature of his job. Tall and slim, his gray hair was always freshly trimmed in a simple cut, and he never appeared unshaven. Remarkably, he also always smelled good. The Old Spice scent had permeated the shop along with oil and rubber.

Jillian laughed. "No, it doesn't. I came by because I want you to check my oil, and I wondered if they towed Stan's car here."

"They did," Grady said. "It's plumb awful. You don't want to see it, Jillian, even if I could show it to you."

"I appreciate your kindness, but it just doesn't seem real. I might have an easier time if I could see his car."

Grady glanced around the garage to make sure they were alone and pointed to the back of his shop behind a row of tires. "I wish you wouldn't, but it's back there. I'm expecting someone specializing in Porsches to pick it up any minute. The police want them to analyze it again even though we examined it last night. The insurance company probably will, too. I don't know what they will find that I can't," he said disgustedly. "They just need to give me a little time."

"I don't either," Jillian agreed. "Do you think it was an accident?"

Grady stopped and stared at her, his blue eyes narrowing. "What makes you ask a question like that?"

"I always thought Stan was a good driver."

"Well, I did, too. It only takes a minute, though, you know," Grady said kindly. "I know this is hard on you, Jillian, but I didn't see any signs of tampering."

"So, nothing like cut brake lines?"

Grady chuckled and leaned against a Toyota. "No, Jillian. You should quit playing detective. No cut brake lines. Just an awful accident."

Although she still found Stan's death odd, Jillian sighed with relief that no one had killed him. Now, she could focus on his financial scam. "Did the cops take anything out of the car?"

Grady looked confused. "Like what?"

"Papers, briefcase, anything like that?"

"They did." Grady appeared even more puzzled. "Why?"

"I think he had some documents from one of my clients. I just hoped they might be at the station."

"The police took a bunch of stuff last night. You might ask them."

"I will. Thanks," Jillian said, despite her sinking heart. If the police had Stan's files at the station, she couldn't examine them. "Do you mind if I see his car for a second?"

"Go ahead, but don't touch anything." Grady sighed and shook his head sadly. "I believe you're making a mistake, but I'll check your oil."

Jillian tiptoed around grease spots until she finally reached Stan's car tucked behind a stack of tires. Their acrid smell, along with a hint of the scent of gasoline, drowned out the Old Spice. The sight took her breath.

Stan's sleek Porsche was reduced to a mangled wreck of metal. He must have had the top down, making the damage even worse. She swallowed her nausea, knowing she had just a couple of minutes to find anything. Grady was bent over her engine, wiping the dipstick on a white paper towel, so Jillian peered into the Porsche. She didn't see any papers or a briefcase. Anything else left probably still littered the ravine.

Another wave of nausea threatened her, and she knew Grady was right. She shouldn't have looked at the car. Jillian sighed and started to turn away when she saw something shining in the gap between the driver's seat and its back. Grady hummed while he worked, and a glance his way showed the back of his head still bent over her engine. Jillian grabbed the silver object with the bottom of her T-shirt, not wanting to leave fingerprints. She stared down in amazement at a thumb drive with the initials SS.

Maybe the flashy accessory had information about his business. She slipped the drive into her pocket and then walked back over to the mechanic.

"Thanks, even though I think it will give me nightmares."

"I warned you." Grady shook a finger at her.

"I know you did. I couldn't imagine how damaged it could be. Without that yellow paint, I wouldn't have recognized it."

"That's why I don't drive convertibles," Grady

grumbled. "Dang things are dangerous. Just get distracted and lose control for a minute and…" He sighed and pointed back at the wreck. "Did you need oil, or did you just want to see his car?" he finished.

Jillian avoided his gaze. "Well, it might have needed oil. A girl can never be too careful."

Grady seemed amused but wiped it away with the back of his greasy hand. "I hope you got some peace from it. Now, you better get along before they come to take the car away." He patted Jillian on her shoulder and handed her the keys to her truck.

"I appreciate it. I've got to get to my office. Thanks again." She left the dark, cool shop and stepped into the sun that promised another hot day.

Jillian knew she should feel bad about what she had done, but the police believed they had gotten all his possessions. Losing the thumb drive could also have lost proof of the fraud. At least, that was how she wanted to justify taking it. She needed to review it before she gave it to the police because she didn't trust Jeff not to file the drive away, never to see the light of day. Sitting behind the wheel, she used a tissue to move the drive from her pocket into a cup holder.

Before she pulled away, she texted Allie and asked if she wanted coffee. Allie shot back a thumbs-up. Jillian remembered Grady's final comment and knew she'd gotten a piece of something, all right. She just couldn't be sure what kind of piece she had found.

Chapter Seven

When Jillian turned the final corner to Kandace's, flashing red, white, and blue lights blinded her, and the sidewalk in front of the coffee shop swarmed with police officers.

Allie jumped out of her Prius, and they ran toward the door together. A baby-faced police officer with a blond buzz cut extended his hand to stop them, but Jillian and Allie pushed past, ignoring his protesting.

Inside the shop, they froze in place. Bits, Bytes, and Brews resembled the path of a Tasmanian devil. Broken glasses, mugs, and spilled sugar made every step crunchy. Tables and chairs tossed everywhere appeared sticky from broken bottles of coffee syrups. Painted graffiti covered the walls with stylized letters and symbols, and Jillian could barely read the words "Hello" and "Gotcha." The spaces that held the laptops and the cash register were all empty.

Officer Gayle Johnson, who had gone to high school a couple of years ahead of Jillian, huddled over Kandace. Friend Gayle was more casual than Officer Johnson, and today, Officer Johnson conducted herself in full police mode, taking notes on a tablet. When Kandace saw Jillian and Allie, she motioned them over. When they reached her, they simultaneously asked, "What happened?"

Kandace brushed tears from her angry, red eyes. "Someone vandalized me!"

Gayle sighed. "I told Kandace about some incidents with a group of high school students from a neighboring town. They spray paint and do minor damage, but their behavior is much worse this time." She closed her eyes and leaned against the table behind her.

Jillian realized Gayle must have been working for hours. "You must be dead on your feet."

"Usually, I love my job," Gayle admitted, "but today, I'm exhausted. I haven't gotten to bed yet." She ran her hand through her curly brown hair. Her short nails had a perfect manicure, burgundy polish setting off her brown skin.

"I'm so sorry," Kandace said. "You've been working on Stan's case all night, right?"

"Our initial examination took several hours, but so far, it appears to be an accident."

"So, Stan just went off the road?" Jillian tried hard to think about anything but the thumb drive.

"It looks that way," Gayle answered. "The news must have shocked you. Regardless of what happened recently, I know you guys had history."

Jillian's cheeks turned hot. "You overheard our last conversation?"

"Only by at least ten people who felt compelled to call the station and remind us. You're just lucky you have a good reputation." She gestured at the other officers. "None of us seriously believed you had anything to do with the accident. And you had an airtight alibi with Penny and Marge."

Jillian stared at her with disbelief, and Gayle nodded. "Yes, we've already checked. Maybe next time you get angry, don't tell someone to drop dead in the middle of a crowd." Gayle winked and wiped her eyes with the palms of her hands.

"I promise. Stan just made me so angry…" Jillian's voice trailed off without knowing what to say next. "But tell me about this." She changed the subject and motioned around at the mess. "Why would anyone want to destroy the coffee shop?"

A loud crash made everyone jump and interrupted Kandace's answer. The four women spun around to see a sheepish employee standing beside an upright table. "Sorry! It fell harder than I expected when I tipped it back upright."

Kandace tempered a sigh with a smile. "No worries, Stu. I guess we're all pretty jumpy." She turned to Jillian. "Bad luck or timing, I guess. I don't think it was directed at me because the vandalism doesn't seem personal. Even the comments on the wall are vague," she continued, and Gayle nodded in agreement. "Still, why target my store?"

"I wish I knew," Gayle admitted. "We've been trying to narrow down the teens involved in the vandalism. Maybe now, more officers can pay attention to the cases."

"I would hope so," Allie growled. Then she looked at Kandace. "What can we do to help?"

"Nothing, right now. The insurance agent should arrive within the hour. At least with my coverage, I won't be out a bunch of money, but I'll need to close for a few days to get cleaned up."

"I bet we can get people to help with that," Jillian said. "I don't understand. You didn't hear anything?" She stared at the damage. How had anyone slept through this?

"No, everything seemed fine when I closed up, but I had a bad headache. You know I get stiff and sore after a busy day. Yesterday, I was on a roll for hours." She glanced at her chair and laughed at her own joke. "When I finally went upstairs, I took a muscle relaxant and went to bed. The teenagers must have arrived after I fell asleep. I didn't know anything until I came down about five this morning." She pointed to the door in the back of the shop that led to her apartment.

"That's scary," Allie said.

Gayle nodded in agreement. "I told her to get an alarm system."

"And cameras," added Kandace. "Yes, I will. At least I lock the elevator every night."

"You lock the stairs, too, right?" Jillian asked.

"I do. I just always felt safe. I never expected vandalism." Her eyes started to fill with tears, but she blinked them back hard.

"You've got tons of friends who will help. Let us know when the insurance people have finished, and we'll get you cleaned up," Jillian promised Kandace.

"I'll do it. Thanks, friends. You'll have to get coffee somewhere else today."

"Just take care of yourself." Jillian and Allie stepped over most of the debris but had to stop on the sidewalk and stamp broken glass and sugar off their shoes. Allie worked extra hard getting everything out of the creases on the soles of her Doc Martins.

"That chaps my assets. I don't understand it."

Jillian's lip twitched at Allie's expression of anger. "I don't know. It doesn't make sense. Hey, I want to talk to you alone. What are you doing today?"

"Repainting a front door for a client. It should only take a couple of hours."

"After you get done, let's go out to the barn. I like the privacy we can have out there. I also need help getting Agatha ready for the parade!"

Allie rolled her eyes. Even in small-town Oklahoma, Allie was a city girl. Her idea of horses was the kind you could ride at the amusement park. But she loved Jillian and was willing to help. "Are you going in those shoes?" she couldn't help but tease, pointing at her friend's flip-flops.

"No, silly. I need to change into boots and older shorts. Want to meet me out there?"

"Sure, Jilly. But why can't you tell me here?"

"I just can't. Come on out after you get done with your project."

Allie's shoulders sank, but then she brightened up. "I'll go there now. I can paint later because the door's in the shade. That way, you can work with Agatha before it gets too hot."

"Perfect. I'll get us some coffee to go. See you in an hour."

Chapter Eight

Back at home, Jillian changed into ratty jean shorts but left on her free T-shirt touting a mutual fund. She added thick white socks to protect her feet from the barn boots she stored beside the door. She knew where they had stepped. While reaching for them, Edgar wormed under her hand for a quick pet. He teased her with ankle rubs and soft chirps, finally talking her out of a snack. A little kibble and a couple of lacings later, she rushed out the door.

Before she put her truck in gear, she took the thumb drive out of the cupholder and dropped it into the center console, not wanting it visible through a window. Just outside town, she pulled into the Grab and Go. She walked past the convenience store's bagged snacks, a tray of donuts, and the hot dog roller. She could never be hungry enough to eat one of those salty pink offerings that smelled like old water.

She poured two coffees, paid the bored teenager handling the cash register, and drove a couple more miles. She grabbed some sips along the way and could feel herself coming back to life.

Finally, she turned down the gravel drive of the stables, her truck brushing cedars that fought for space on the lane. As she pulled her truck onto the gravel patch that created a makeshift parking lot, she laughed.

Somehow, Allie again beat her to their destination.

Jillian pulled her truck beside the hybrid and walked around the back to open the Ford's lid. Four bales of hay and a bag of grain filled the bed. Allie got out and joined her friend, and they walked to get the wheelbarrow. "Okay, Jilly, your work can wait a few minutes. Nobody can hear us except for a few horses. Talk to me."

"Remember, you can't share this with anyone."

Allie flattened her lips together, creating a furrow between her eyebrows. "You know I wouldn't."

Jillian gave her a quick hug. "But remember, that includes Penny." Agatha trotted up to them when they got to her run. They each gave her a cookie, and Jillian grabbed the wheelbarrow and headed back to her truck with it.

"Don't freak me out like that," complained Allie. "Just tell me what you've done."

"Well, I went to Grady's garage this morning. I thought the police might have taken Stan's car there, and I wanted to see it."

"Oh, lemon drops! Why would you want to do that?"

Despite the heat, Jillian shuddered. "Yeah, that car damage was the stuff of nightmares. I went because I wondered if Stan's belongings were still in it."

"Why did you think they would tow it to Grady's? The news report didn't say anything about him last night."

"Gayle's taken her car there for years, and I saw her on the news report. Also, I couldn't imagine they would take the car to a chain store with a rotating cast of employees, and Grady's seemed like the best choice on a short list."

"Smart," approved Allie. "Still, I can't imagine any papers surviving that roll. You saw the car on the news last night and, apparently, in person today. And not only that, why wouldn't the police have taken everything?" Allie asked.

"Right," Jillian interrupted Allie when she stopped to breathe. "The papers should have been at the station or down in the ravine, but the police missed a thumb drive wedged between the front seat and its back."

Allie's expressive blue eyes widened almost to the size of her face, and her deeply arched brown eyebrows raised almost to her hairline. Then her eyes narrowed.

"What did you do?"

"I took it." Jillian stared at the bed of her truck while she pulled out the first bale of hay.

"What?" Allie screeched. "Why did you do that?"

Jillian couldn't meet her friend's gaze. "I hope I can prove whether or not Stan was stealing."

"Shinola! You tampered with evidence, and you stole something!"

"Stan's car isn't a crime scene! You heard Gayle say he just went off the road," insisted Jillian. "I know the wreck doesn't make sense, but even if it wasn't an accident, the police missed the drive. We would have lost the data if I hadn't taken it."

"But still…"

"I'll give it to them after I've looked at it." Jillian stacked the hay in front of Agatha's run, sweat streaming down her face.

"Be careful. Your love of mysteries will catch up with you. I hate what you did, but can I see it, too?"

"Sure." Jillian was relieved that Allie at least pretended to understand. "Don't get too excited, though, because it might have nothing useful. Either way, I want to find something that proves Stan's guilt or innocence. I was going to open it this morning on one of Kandace's computers because she has every kind of protective software you could imagine, but you know how that ended."

"Why not at your house?"

"Because I have enough information on my laptop to steal someone's identity. What if Stan picked up a virus on the drive? He isn't a testimony for good decision-making, and I can't risk my clients' data." Jillian walked back to her truck for the last bale. Allie's legs were shorter than her friend's, and she jogged to keep up, her face turning red from the heat and exertion. Allie liked her air conditioning.

Jillian heard the artist pant for breath. "I'm sorry. Only one more to go. You okay?"

"I'll be fine unless I have a heatstroke." She laughed, but Jillian knew she wasn't kidding. Her friend continued, "You know, I could help you with the data. Kandace doesn't have any computers now, but I have one."

Jillian looked appreciatively at her friend. "But what about your getting hacked?"

"What would they get? I don't bank on my computer. I bank on my phone. I take credit cards on my phone. I do everything through an app. Maybe they can hack my social media, but I'll keep an eye on that." She grinned at Jillian. "If you're the detective, I'll be your sidekick."

"I can't imagine anyone I'd rather have at my side." Jillian sighed with relief as she arranged the last hay bale on the stack. Sweat poured down her body while her horse stretched her neck over the fence, trying to reach a bite.

Jillian reached across the fence and rubbed the red mare on her nose. "What, pretty girl? All that hay in your manger doesn't taste as good as the new stuff? What do you think, Agatha? Should we use Allie's computer to open the thumb drive? I don't want to put her in danger."

Agatha nodded her head up and down, either agreeing with Jillian or trying to reach more hay. The friends burst into laughter.

"Well, Agatha thinks we should proceed," Jillian announced.

"I need to paint this afternoon, but maybe tomorrow?"

"Sure," Jillian said and grabbed Agatha's halter. "In the meantime, once we rest for a minute, do you have more time today?"

"A little, why?" Allie asked, running her fingers through her spiky hair, leaving it standing up in wet clumps.

"The 4th of July parade comes in a few days." Allie nodded. "Remember when the horse ran away last year?"

"Yes," Allie answered slowly. "It was all everyone talked about for days. So scary! At least it ran straight down the road and not into the crowd, that poor young rider hanging on for dear life and trying to make it slow down. I remember all those little kids standing right by the horses. When it finally stopped, didn't she fall off and break her arm?"

Jillian nodded. "She did. The whole situation was awful and could have ended much worse. I don't want Agatha pulling a stunt like that. I don't think she would, but I haven't ridden her in public for a while. I want to spook her a little out here and see what she does."

"Okaaay," Allie reluctantly agreed, stretching out her response. "What, exactly, do you want me to do?"

"While I'm riding her in the arena, I want you to try to scare her. Wave this grocery bag at her, whoop, holler, and throw your arms in the air."

Allie's brows furrowed more, and she shook her head vigorously side to side. "Why would you want me to do that? She might throw you off."

"I don't think so, but I know that one person with a plastic bag will be less scary than hundreds of screaming kids on the parade route."

After Jillian tacked up Agatha with her beautiful rose-carved leather saddle, she led her to the outdoor arena. Then she swung her leg over and asked for a few steps. After the stress of the last twenty-four hours, each footfall seemed to clear Jillian's head a little more. They moved at different speeds, walking, trotting, and loping.

With alert ears and easy yielding to Jillian's leg, Agatha seemed to enjoy herself, but the real test was still to come.

"Okay, Allie, I want you to wave the bag while we ride by you. And cheer for us, too. Make a lot of noise."

"I don't like this, Jilly."

"Don't worry. With any luck, Agatha will ignore the whole thing."

The loop around the arena started well enough, but as Jillian and Agatha approached Allie, she waved the bag. Agatha pinned her ears and stepped sideways but continued. Then Allie started yelling and cheering, and Agatha began to pick up the pace. Jillian sat back a little, released her leg, and the horse slowed to a walk and finished the circle.

When Agatha should have responded better the second time around, she decided the waving bag was the scariest monster ever. She took off across the middle of the arena like her tail was on fire. Jillian hunkered down in the saddle and pulled one of the reins hard. It worked a little too well, and Agatha stopped cold.

With Jillian's balance off center, she slid off and landed in the soft dirt. Allie screamed while her owner's unexpected dismount got Agatha's attention. The horse turned around, walked over to Jillian, and sniffed her cap. Then she stood there until Jillian laughed. "You're asking me what I'm doing down here on the ground?" Agatha nodded or shooed a fly and then dropped her head again in apology.

"Serves me right for being too busy at work to spend enough time out here," Jillian admitted. "Okay, pretty girl. I'll make you a higher priority. We'll work a lot more before the parade."

"Oh, I'm so sorry!" Allie said. "I shouldn't have listened to you. Did you hurt yourself?"

Jillian stood and brushed the dirt off. "No, but I'd rather fall here in the soft dirt than on the street, and that wreck would have been a disaster during the parade. You did exactly what I asked, but we need more practice." Agatha slipped her head over Jillian's shoulder and nodded up and down, agreeing or rubbing an itchy cheek against her owner's hair.

"I'll come out here every day if you need," promised Allie.

"Thanks, friend, but no more waving dragon bags under saddle today. I'll show her they can't kill her from the ground. You go, get out of the heat. I'm going to rest a minute and then do some easy walking and trotting. We'll try riding with the bags again tomorrow."

Chapter Nine

Once Allie stopped waving the bag, Agatha acted like a perfect angel. Jillian rode another half hour and then worked her on a lunge line from the ground, waving the dragon bag and asking the red horse to trot in a large circle. Agatha acted like she saw flapping bags daily and listened to everything her owner asked. Jillian decided to quit while she was ahead, cooled Agatha with a hose, and drove home.

After a quick shower, herself, to wash off the sweat and dirt, Jillian finally sat down on the cool smoothness of her brown leather sofa. Thank goodness for air conditioning. She had just put her bare feet on the wooden coffee table when her cell phone rang. The caller ID photo showed Penny holding an enormous bouquet of sunflowers.

"Jillian, I'm so sorry about Stan. No matter how you feel about him now, with your history, his death has to hurt."

Jillian's eyes stung with tears again. "More than I expected," she admitted, "especially in light of everything else."

"Have you heard anything today? I saw the story on the late news last night, and they mentioned it again this morning but didn't have any more information."

Jillian trusted Penny completely but had already

taken a risk telling Allie about the thumb drive. "Gayle told me they think Stan got distracted and drove off the road," she finally offered.

"You know more than you're saying." Jillian could imagine Penny's eyes never leaving hers.

She moved uncomfortably in her chair, glad to be on the phone so she didn't have to meet Penny's gaze. "Not really," she said weakly.

Penny laughed. "I love you, but I don't believe you. I also know about the thumb drive and want to see the documents. I don't care much about Stan's business, but I want to see that he didn't steal from Marge and that she is okay. I'll bring snacks," she bribed.

"What? Oh, Allie," Jillian yelped. Edgar loved to sleep beside a stack of mystery books on the piñon wood mantel of her white stucco fireplace. When Jillian raised her voice, he leaped down, trotted over, jumped on the couch beside her, and glanced up with a quizzical look on his face.

"Child, you know that girl can't keep a secret. We're all living examples of how rumors spread in small towns."

"That's the truth. She didn't waste any time calling."

"I've known for about an hour. I just wanted to give you a chance to take a shower. What do you think you'll find on the thumb drive?"

Now curled in a ball, Edgar heard Penny's question. He glanced around with one sleepy eye, almost shrugged, and went to sleep.

Jillian stroked his soft fur. "I'm afraid Stan may have used new funds he received to pay off existing clients who wanted money. He also may have spent a lot of what people believed he invested. I hope I'm wrong, but he may not have much money left."

"Oh, my goodness. You think Stan was running a Ponzi scheme?"

Penny Kroll was a powerhouse. "Impressive."

"No, I just love finance. Can you believe I read a great book about Charles Ponzi last year, the man whose antics provided the name? Do you know the story?" she asked.

"Only the basics," Jillian admitted. Penny needed no more encouragement.

"Well, Charles Ponzi lived in the early twentieth century in Boston. He needed to raise money, so he got investors by promising high rates of return. But his gains weren't the result of skill. Instead, he paid existing clients with funds he received from new victims."

Curious, Jillian sat up a little more on her couch. "How did they catch him?"

"Eventually, the *Boston Post* investigated Ponzi because they doubted his claims. Federal authorities arrested him on August 12, 1920, and charged him with mail fraud."

"Mail fraud?"

"Uh-huh," Penny said. "He used the mail service to transport important pieces of his crime, like letters that gave investment returns. Mail fraud law provides a useful way to charge thieves and fraudsters. By the time of his custody, Ponzi had stolen about seven million."

"What a lot of money, especially back then," Jillian said. "I hope he went to prison for a long time."

"Fourteen years."

"That's not long," Jillian growled.

"I agree. I guess that's why we have the expression, 'white-collar crime pays,' " Penny said.

"If I ever have questions about financial cons, I'll have to consult you!" Penny laughed, and Jillian continued. "But Stan can't defend himself, and I don't want to accuse him of something he didn't do. I've got to try to find another explanation."

"That's what I love about you, child," Penny said. "You're always fair even when you get on a cause."

"I don't go on frequent crusades," Jillian protested.

"No, but when you do, you take no prisoners. Your grandmother would be proud of you. I'll let you go. Everybody wants to talk to me. Just now, I've missed several calls."

Jillian paused. "It sounds ghoulish to worry about money now that Stan has died."

"Maybe a little, but you've got to get to the bottom of it or just turn it over to the regulators."

"I'll talk to them after I know a little more. Recently, everybody's short-staffed, and I hate to offer a vague complaint." Jillian could almost hear Penny's head nodding through the phone.

"Smart," the woman said. "Let's see what's there first. Allie told me she was coming over for dinner at your house tomorrow. I could bring dessert," she bribed.

Edgar raised his head hopefully at the talk of food, but after nothing yummy to eat arrived, he yawned, his white teeth bright against his shiny blue-black fur. Then he curled up tighter and closed his eyes.

"I'd love dessert! Allie wanted to come today, but she needs to finish painting a door this evening. I dragged her out to the barn earlier."

"So I heard," laughed Penny. "You okay?"

"Only hurt my pride. I don't know what got into Agatha. Poor Allie. I think my fall scared her to death.

That girl likes nothing concerning the outdoors. I'm glad you'll be here when we open the drive. You may recognize some names if we find anything."

"I hope not, but I'd love to help. What time?"

"Say six?" Jillian asked. "Also, have you heard anything about Stan's funeral? I don't think he has any family here. Who's going to organize it?"

"I don't know. Unless they do an autopsy, I think the details will come out by tomorrow. No one could have survived in that mangled wreck of a car. I don't think his cause of death is in question."

The image of the yellow Porsche flooded Jillian's mind, and her eyes prickled again. "What an awful way to die. I'll see you tomorrow."

After she hung up, she sat staring off into space. Had Stan's wreck happened because of carelessness, or was she right about his con, and had someone else figured it out and sought justice that didn't require regulators? And what about Kandace's vandalism? Was that related to Stan's accident? Kandace wouldn't have taken revenge on him all these years later, would she? No, of course not. Kandace wouldn't hurt anyone.

Frustrated with her suspicions and too many options, Jillian realized she was hungry. She slid off her leather couch and opened the side-by-side freezer. Edgar beat her there, so he could stick his nose into the cold air, examining the shelves for his options.

She pulled out a frozen chicken breast and some broccoli and showed them to Edgar, who sniffed the meat and ignored the vegetables. She opened her cupboard and found Italian seasoning. She twisted off the lid, and the smell of garlic and oregano confirmed her decision. If she got it in the oven now, she'd eat in an hour.

She poured some red wine and sat back down to wait. Outside her window, she could see lightning to the west. She watched the clouds light up pink and white from within, and occasionally, a jagged white line streaked to the ground.

Chapter Ten

The following morning, thunder woke Jillian before her alarm clock. She lay in the dark as bright flashes punctuated everything, even through her closed eyes. Edgar snuggled up tighter against her with each boom. The usually brave little cat hated thunderstorms.

The pouring rain made her grateful that she paid a friend from the barn to feed Agatha twice a day. Although she loved her horse, sometimes her schedule wouldn't let her get out there on time. On days like today, she appreciated the help.

After attempting to go back to sleep for an hour, Jillian's whirling mind forced her to give up and get out of bed. Edgar closed his eyes and curled tight against the pillow. He would take a pass on the stormy morning.

She padded to the kitchen and made half a pot of coffee. The individual-cup makers held no attraction for her because she drank too many of them. Jillian didn't measure her coffee consumption in cups; she measured it in pots, and her one-month pod attempt cost a hundred dollars. She assumed they worked well for people who drank a cup a day.

Although the worst of the storm had passed, lightning still slashed across the dim morning sky, and thunder rumbled. She poured cereal into a green Fiestaware bowl and coffee into a coordinating red cup.

While she ate, Jillian checked the local news on her phone, wondering if Stan's wreck still captured the public's attention. She couldn't find anything directly; however, an editorial mentioned the accident and the dangerous curve in the road. The author argued how the Magnolia Hill City Council should consider making that stretch of highway safer.

In Oklahoma, small communities make great use of their state highways. Unlike the major thoroughfares of larger towns, however, these less traveled roads often consisted of two lanes of questionable condition. Jillian didn't believe an ordinance would have saved Stan, but a safer stretch of highway would certainly be nice.

By the time she finished her breakfast and headed to work, the rain had stopped entirely. The oppressive humidity from the overnight storms showed itself in the steam that formed on her windshield where the air conditioning hit. She pulled to the curb in front of her office and saw several bikes already chained to the old hitching posts that had been repurposed. Magnolia Hill valued its past and incorporated it whenever possible.

The streets had come to life after the storm. The diner next door already had a long line, and Jillian could smell the bacon, frying potatoes, and pancakes. Her nose tried to direct her feet, but she didn't need to begin the day with a million calories and carbs. Plus, she'd already eaten a bowl of cereal.

She unlocked her office and went into the breakroom to start another pot of coffee. She opened the fridge, got out a blueberry yogurt, and peeled off the lid without enthusiasm. Biscuits and gravy sounded better.

Once at her desk with yogurt and spoon in hand, Jillian saw that Nancy had called late the day before.

When she called her client back, the phone rang four times, and Nancy picked it up right before it went to her voicemail.

"Thank you for calling me." The older woman sounded near tears. "I'm sorry. I was so embarrassed to contact you that I almost didn't answer my phone. But now that Stan's died, I didn't know who else to call."

Jillian felt enormous sympathy for her despair. "I promised you could call me the last time we talked."

"You must hate me for dropping you after all you've done for me. And now I have to ask if you can help me again."

"I don't hate you, Nancy. Of course, I'll try to help. I just hope your transfer hasn't gone through yet." Jillian turned on her computer and waited for it to power up. Although the laptop screen usually popped right up, today, the process seemed excruciatingly slow.

"I don't know. I met with Stan a couple of days before I talked to you. I knew you'd notice the account, so I called," the older woman explained, her voice still shaking.

Jillian slumped, looking sadly at Katherine's empty chair and desk. Her assistant defined the word "organized." Every night, she cleared her desk of all finished work and laid anything she hadn't done in a neat pile in the corner. Then she washed her Galveston coffee cup and set it beside the picture of her young daughter.

Nothing got by Katherine. She always tracked incoming and outgoing transfers daily, but while she was on vacation, Jillian was supposed to check. The planner sighed. She must have missed it.

She skimmed through the software's data, and sure enough, Nancy's account had been drained of funds.

However, the list of transactions had no transfer notification. Confused, Jillian asked, "Nancy, did Stan transfer you to another custodian?"

"I don't know what you mean by that."

"I mean, did he open another account somewhere else?" Jillian named a couple of widely advertised investment firms, and Nancy interrupted her.

"No, he said he didn't do it that way. He asked me to withdraw the funds and write him a check."

"You wrote him a check? How did you take the distribution if I didn't help you do it?" Jillian put the phone on speaker so she could type with both hands, and started searching in her software for clues about the transfer.

"Stan told me to call the number on the bottom of your statement and tell them I wanted my money. Once they asked a few questions to identify me, they sold my holdings and wired the money to my bank account. After that, I wrote the check to Stan."

Jillian could tell by her client's explanation that she saw nothing unusual in Stan's actions. At the same time, the planner tried to keep her growing rage at Stan from showing in her voice. Maybe the money was safely deposited somewhere. Until she knew, she didn't want to panic the older woman. "You wrote him a check?"

Sniffling became outright crying. "I'm so sorry. I feel like I let you down."

"Please don't cry," Jillian said more evenly than she felt. "I'll try to help you fix it. Do you know if Stan cashed it?"

"He did. Right before he died."

Now, anger ran down Jillian's legs until she felt her feet going numb. Sure enough. Stan stole money just like

Ponzi.

"Nancy, I need to make a couple of phone calls to check our next steps since Stan's office isn't likely open. Even if his assistant Betty wants to help his clients, I'm sure a plan needs to be developed."

The image of Betty flying down the road in Stan's car flashed through Jillian's mind again. If the Porsche had been tampered with, the assistant had been lucky that the car hadn't malfunctioned while she was driving it. Unless she was the one who did the tampering, Jillian thought darkly. She brushed that theory aside and turned her attention to her client again.

"It doesn't matter. Betty can't help. I'm sorry," Nancy whimpered.

"Why can't Betty help?" Jillian didn't even want to ask. Everything the older woman said made the situation worse.

"Stan met me for dinner the night I wrote him the check. He told me that he took care of opening client accounts, himself. Something about Betty not holding the right securities license, so she couldn't accept funds."

"You never talked to Betty?"

"No. Stan told me to call him on his cell phone if I had any questions. I'm sorry. Did I do something wrong?"

Jillian managed a "No," but her anger at Stan had her head buzzing so loudly she almost couldn't concentrate.

Her clients knew Katherine as well as they knew her. They wouldn't think anything about talking with her about something they needed. She wondered if Betty had met any of Stan's clients, or was she just a prop in his elaborate scheme? Or, worse yet, did she help him launder the money?

"Do you even have Stan's office phone number?"

"Well, I guess I could find it, but Stan gave me his card with his cell printed on it. He told me that was the easiest way to contact him. I've never called his office."

"How did you find him originally?"

"I didn't. He phoned me. I knew he made great returns for several of my friends, and they gave him my number. He called and invited all of us to join him at Ebony and Ivory for dinner. Over filet mignon, he told me that he had a proprietary system that helped him anticipate the stock market's direction. He also explained how he could make money in both up-and-down markets. I'm sorry—he even claimed you couldn't earn good returns because you didn't understand the details of investing like he did. After talking to him and my friends that night, I thought I'd make more money if I hired him. I'm so sorry."

Jillian knew if he had taken the group to Ebony and Ivory, he'd laid it on thick. She loved the restaurant but went there rarely for special occasions. No wonder Nancy believed he could earn her more money. When Jillian turned her head from side to side, she heard a loud crack and wondered how much more stress her body could take. "Don't worry, Nancy. I'll see what I can do."

An apologetic, weeping Nancy hung up the phone.

Jillian walked around her office, trying to get control of her anger. Usually, her many pictures of Agatha helped put her in a better mood, but now, photos of them riding in parades just added to her stress. Out her window, the massive clouds rebuilding in the west matched her mood. She knew she needed to talk to Betty as soon as possible. She also needed to see the data on that thumb drive. Maybe she could find where Stan had moved the money.

In the meantime, she should check further into Stan's background. If he had not opened Nancy's account legally, she wondered if there had been trouble with the financial regulators previously. She knew she would need to call the Department of Securities soon, but she rationalized that since Stan was dead, he couldn't do any more damage. And she wanted answers sooner than she believed they could provide.

Jillian typed brokercheck.finra.org in her laptop's browser. She should have checked Stan's financial background earlier, but the stress of the last few days had been overwhelming. When she typed in his name, she was more disturbed by what she didn't see than what she found.

The site showed Stan's work and regulatory history in Texas, and his record showed no bad behavior. Either he was very clever or hadn't committed any illegal acts there. However, Stan had no history of working in financial services in Oklahoma. According to the site, Stan had left the industry. With this new information, Jillian's head pounded like it would explode, and she knew she needed to call the Oklahoma Department of Securities. Everything Stan did in Magnolia Hill was a con, and his accident seemed even more suspicious. Who had figured it out?

Chapter Eleven

Jillian poured another cup of coffee into the mug with Agatha's picture and continued to pace back and forth in her empty lobby, trying to decide what to do next. If Stan had stolen Nancy's money, Penny's friends were likely victims, too. And if the authorities couldn't find the money, what in the world would his clients do? Even those with modest means rocked an active, vibrant retirement lifestyle. For the many widows, the money they gave Stan resulted from two lifetimes of work. If their funds were gone, they would never financially recover.

She recalled Marge, her kitty, and their tidy but simple home. Marge didn't have much money, and losing it would ruin her. Tears began to run down Jillian's cheeks, and she couldn't bear to think about the damage any longer. She needed to look at that thumb drive. She packed her briefcase, grabbed her purse, and headed for her truck.

Finally home, she opened her front door, and Edgar ran to meet her, meowing for an unexpected lunch. She opened a can of food and called Allie while she put it in his bowl.

"I hear I'm making dinner for you and Penny." She laughed. "Do you want pasta salad? I love it this time of year because I don't want to put anything in the oven."

"Sounds good. With artichokes?"

"Of course, with artichokes. Could you bring a loaf of sourdough from Bob's Bakery? Penny promised dessert."

After Jillian hung up the phone, she went into the kitchen and started boiling the water. First, she needed to prepare the pasta and get it in the fridge to chill. Then she pulled out a package of cubed ham, shredded cheese, black olive slices, artichoke hearts, and Italian dressing. She grabbed an onion from her pantry and chopped it with the artichokes.

Once she had the salad in the fridge, she sat on the couch with her phone. Edgar jumped up beside her, and she petted his head. "Come on, kitty, let's find some dirt on Stan." The black cat meowed vigorously and sniffed her screen before he lay down.

Jillian thought reviewing Stan's social media accounts might prove useful, and she was relieved that he let anyone see his feed. She started with his Facebook images and found that he and the blonde from the coffee shop appeared to have a history. He didn't post many pictures, but a few showed them standing together, usually at business events. One image revealed the name of a hotel in Dallas, and Jillian wondered if they knew each other when Stan worked there.

He had no other social media accounts, so she studied his website. Again, nothing popped up. His online presence seemed as boring as his car was ostentatious. Maybe he didn't want to draw too much attention to himself outside Magnolia Hill. Jillian thought if she were running a con, she would want to appear dull to anyone outside it.

The afternoon went quickly, and by the time Allie

rang the bell, Jillian had chilled the pasta and transferred a bagged tossed salad into a pretty, Navajo bowl. Finally, she put Bob's sourdough on a breadboard, poured Allie a pinot grigio, and invited her to sit on the couch while they waited for Penny.

"Didn't you paint this afternoon? How are you so clean?" Jillian asked.

Allie shook her head hard, and little water droplets flew. "I was hot, dusty, and paint-covered an hour ago. I didn't dare sit on your furniture dressed like that, so I cleaned up. Seriously, how do you keep it so nice?"

Jillian glanced around the room at the hardwood floors, southwest rugs, and fireplace. Edgar sat on his favorite piñon perch again, and when Allie made eye contact with him, he offered a cheerful meow that made Allie giggle.

Jillian answered. "Hardwood cleans up easier than carpet, and I shake the rugs every week. The leather couch and chairs just need to be wiped down, and any spills clean up easier than off upholstery."

"Well, it wouldn't last a week at my condo," Allie said. "I prefer a style that some call early garage sale—cheap, and I don't have to worry about it. If the furniture gets a little extra paint, it doesn't matter."

Jillian wanted to disagree with her, but Allie's taste in furniture leaned toward useful and eclectic. Eclectic sounded so much better than mismatched. Instead of responding, she got out salad bowls and silverware. She finished the last place setting just as the doorbell rang.

Penny practically bounced through the doorway. "Girls, you won't believe what I found out!"

"What?" they asked.

"Get me a glass of wine, and I'll tell you all I know,"

she teased. She slipped off her sensible, black loafers because the rain had finally started in earnest. Once Penny sat on the couch with a generous pour of pinot, Jillian also brought her glass in. Then she sat in the oversized leather chair that faced Penny and Allie.

"Okay—tell us what you found out."

"Stan's wife is making his funeral plans." Penny stretched out the sentence, knowing she had caught both younger women by surprise. A great crash of thunder accentuated her words.

"Wife?"

"Yes, wife. They haven't lived together much since he moved back to Magnolia Hill, but they're very much married."

Jillian shook her head in disbelief. Stan didn't seem like the marrying kind. "Separated?"

"Not apparently. I heard from reliable sources at the beauty parlor that she has a job in Tulsa. They've kept a commuter marriage."

"So, Stan doesn't even want to live here? He only trolls for clients in Magnolia Hill?" Jillian said with disgust. That tied to Nancy's experience with him.

"Maybe. Stan never acted like a small-town guy," agreed Allie. "He thought he was too good for all of us."

Penny continued. "And according to the lowdown from the nail tech, she's a stunner, very country club." Penny had a self-satisfied smirk. She loved sharing new, juicy gossip.

"Oh gracious, I've seen her," Jillian said. "She came in with Stan when I crashed into him in the coffee shop."

Penny chuckled. "I heard about your run-in with Stan today, too. Fortunately, the Blow-Dry Caucus knows that you wouldn't hurt a soul. I didn't have to come to your defense, not that I wouldn't." Penny blew Jillian a kiss. "Tell me about this woman."

"Very put together. Mid-length, blonde hair overly teased."

"Not a fan of 'big hair,' " interrupted Allie. "Too retro and artificial."

"But it's all the rage in some circles," Jillian defended, feeling sorry for the recently widowed woman. "It has been for years." She pointed at Allie. "We only saw her for a minute, but she was a little taller than Stan and model thin, with a taste for designer shoes." Jillian could spot nice shoes from a mile away, and the Manolo Blahnik sandals stood out from the more common flip-flops and sneakers at Kandace's. "What's her name?" she asked Penny.

"Gina. The caucus couldn't settle on her last name, but it starts with a G and might sound German."

"She didn't take Stan's last name?"

"Jilly, if you could avoid having a last name of Savage, wouldn't you do it?" Penny asked.

Jillian laughed. "I would. You can tell me after the funeral if you think she's pretty. I can't beat you for news, but I got information today, myself." She caught them up on everything Nancy said.

"For all the world, Stan appears to be a scammer," Jillian said. "If so, most of his clients will have lost all the money they gave them."

"Fudge muffins! Even your last client?" Allie asked.

"Even Nancy. Stan convinced her to sell everything and move the money to the bank before she told me. Then she wrote him a personal check that emptied her account."

"Oh no," Penny said. "Poor Nancy. Poor Marge."

Jillian took a sip of her wine. "It gets worse. Stan wasn't legally registered as a financial adviser in Oklahoma."

"So, no chance he's just an idiot? You think he's a thief?" Allie asked.

"Everything points to that. A few years ago, he had a legit practice in Texas, which gave him knowledge and the ability to gain his new clients' confidence. But I'm not stunned he wanted money. Ever since high school, Stan loved the easy buck. He just doesn't seem capable of pulling off something this complicated."

"Jilly, sometimes, people appear more clever than smart," Penny said.

Allie chimed in. "I remember how Stan could get out of doing his homework in high school."

When Jillian returned to get the pasta and tossed salad, she recalled again how Stan talked her into doing his assignments for him. He always created a convincing reason why he couldn't finish—interfering football practice, running errands for his folks, so many excuses.

Sometimes, he didn't bother creating a reason and told her that he didn't understand what the teacher wanted. Each time, his story sounded similar. "You're so smart. Can you help me?" he would ask. "Please? I just don't understand, and you always seem to know what the teacher means." His blue eyes with long lashes never blinked until she said yes.

Then she would carefully review the questions with him, explaining the correct answers, but the puzzled expression never left his face. She deserved most of his high school diploma.

"Jilly? Jilly? Where did you go?" Allie's voice brought her back to reality.

Jillian took another sip of her wine. "Oh, just thinking back on Stan when he was younger. Even then, he could game the system."

"Uh-huh," Allie said flatly. She hadn't liked Stan in high school. Even then, she hung out with artists, and they gave a suspicious eye to anyone whose lifestyle ran too far inside social trends. Jillian knew Stan's country club clothing and fashionable hair didn't appeal to her friend then or now.

On the other hand, Allie's high school boyfriend, Ace, wore a lot of black, even down to his nail polish. Despite his goth appearance, Ace was all right. When her truck got stuck in the mud at the barn, Stan didn't have time to pull it out. But Ace arrived in half an hour, right after Allie called and told him that Jillian needed to be rescued. The couple pushed away at the back of her truck, somehow laughing at the fine spray of mud covering them when she accelerated. Allie and Ace—always there when you needed them. Jillian was sorry they broke up.

"You're lost in thought again," Allie said.

"Don't get mad. Ace always was a great guy."

Allie sighed. "Yeah, I think he's still pretty cool. I wish we'd stayed together, but the timing didn't work out…" Allie trailed off, and Jillian didn't push the conversation.

"Enough of the past, girls," Penny declared. "First, we eat, and then we've got to open that thumb drive."

Chapter Twelve

After they had finished the pasta and bread, Allie pulled her computer out of her backpack while Jillian got the thumb drive out of her purse and then went to the kitchen for the tray of Penny's brownies. "You outdid yourself," she said, cutting through the fudgy cake covered with chocolate and mint icing.

"Thanks, I made them this afternoon." She picked up the metal thumb drive with a tissue and turned it over in her hand. "Fancy. Those initials pretty much seal the deal, don't they?"

Jillian nodded.

"How did you… What did you… Never mind, I don't want to know." Penny laughed as she set down the drive, pushed back her red Fiestaware plate, and wiped her mouth with a matching napkin.

"You probably don't," Jillian agreed.

"Why not just turn the drive over to the police?" the older woman asked. "You know Gayle will be angry for keeping this from her."

"Yeah, I know. If I can't find something quickly, I will," Jillian explained. "But because I'm trying to find financial information, I think I might recognize it more than they would. I'm sure Officer Stone wouldn't listen to me anyway. I'd hate to lose information that might explain what happened."

"No, Jeff's too by the book to appreciate your involvement in his investigation," laughed Penny.

"And Gayle shouldn't argue with him directly if we can help her avoid it. The relationship could get awkward since they're partners," Allie agreed around a mouthful of brownie. She swallowed hard. "Okay, let's see what we've got. I'll run a quick virus check on the device before we open anything." Jillian used a yellow napkin that had matched her plate to hand the thumb drive to Allie.

"Here, I want to avoid getting our fingerprints on it."

Allie studied the drive. "Looks like we'll avoid more than that. Is that blood?" She pointed to a brownish-red stain on the bottom of the silver block.

"Eeww. I hope not. Anyhow, don't touch it," advised Jillian. She didn't want Allie to get cold feet now.

Allie put the drive in the side of her laptop and started the virus check. The three women watched the program end, and Allie opened the device.

"Sheesh, Stan had a bunch of folders," she said.

"I wonder if this is a backup of his whole system or where he stored private information," mused Jillian.

Penny glanced up from her fork to Jillian. "I still don't know how you got this."

"I found it." Jillian focused on licking mint off of her finger.

"Uh-huh." Penny reviewed the open directory of folders. "Look, girls, he kept an image folder. I don't think I want to see his pictures." She raised her eyebrows at Jillian and Allie, and they laughed.

"Brace yourself, Penny. We should still check," Jillian said. "Go ahead," she encouraged Allie.

Stan's photos didn't have any obscene or frightening content. They included Stan and Gina on the beach, laughing with arms around each other.

Jillian felt a sharp pang of sympathy from the image. She couldn't imagine the pain Stan's wife must feel now that he was dead. They must have cared a lot for each other. Poor Gina.

Other pictures were more business-related. In one set, Stan wore a navy blazer and held a glass of red wine as he stood in a group of other people dressed professionally. Finally, they saw Stan's collection of overly posed headshots. Jillian recognized several images from his website. Unfortunately, none appeared to offer valuable insights, so Allie clicked it shut to review other folders.

"Oh, he has travel documents," said Allie. "Let's check them out." When she opened it, they saw boarding passes, electronic cruise tickets, confirmations for hotels, and websites for tourist attractions in New York, the Caymans, Cozumel, Costa Rica, and other places.

"I don't think these travel documents matter," she said, looking at Jillian and Penny. When neither objected, she closed it and went on to the next one.

"This folder has the updates for his Porsche," she continued.

"Updates for his Porsche?" Penny asked. She had put on red half glasses to read easier, and she glanced at the two younger women over the top of them.

"New cars require software updates. We can review them, but I don't think we'll find anything useful." Allie clicked on the folder. "See, they are just files that would update his car." She closed it again.

"Good grief," Penny said. "I like technology, but I

don't want to have to update my car."

"It improves syncing functions, maps, that kind of thing," explained Allie. "He didn't hide client files here. You can tell by the file extension. They're specific to cars." Penny and Jillian stared at her, surprised. "What? I talk to Will once in a while. He's told me about them."

"Why did you talk to Will?" Jillian asked in amazement.

"I try to get some publicity in the newspaper for art shows. He helps me."

"Better you than me," Jillian said. "Will Anderson may know a lot about cars, but he'll never let you forget it."

"Oh, come on, Jillian. Don't start with Will again."

"Seriously?" Jillian snorted.

"I know you think he didn't work hard enough in college, but he still graduated with honors," Allie reminded.

"But he still got his daddy to give him a job at the newspaper. Must be useful to have a father who is the chief editor."

"True," Penny said sadly. "But maybe he also felt he had to go to work for his father's paper. In any case, I'm surprised you dislike him so much." Her voice held a touch of criticism, and she glanced at her granddaughter, who nodded in agreement.

"Well, I do," Jillian said defensively, hating that she had upset Penny. "His taking advantage of family connections is only part of why I don't respect him, but let's not go into it when we have work to do." She focused on the files. "Check it out. Open that folder labeled 'Savage Special.' "

Allie clicked the name, and files covered her screen.

"Bingo!" Jillian crowed.

Stan had at least twenty-five folders labeled with last names organized alphabetically. Jillian skimmed down until she saw Nancy's folder. "Let me see the mouse." At the word "mouse," Edgar jumped on the table. Everyone laughed at the little cat as he sniffed around, checking for crumbs. Even though Jillian knew he shouldn't sit where she ate, she left him alone until he curled up in the far corner so that he could watch them.

When she found the documents in Nancy's folder, Jillian groaned. One provided the amount of money Nancy had given to Stan, followed by the bank routing and account numbers. He also had a copy of her investment statements, information on another bank account, her driver's license and Social Security card, and an image of her signature.

"Anything useful, Jilly?" Allie asked as she stole another brownie. When Jillian raised her eyebrows, she said, "Stress makes me hungry."

"Fair enough. It looks pretty damning. Stan had everything he would need to steal Nancy's identity and maybe help himself to money from other accounts. I wonder if he was going to forge her signature. Why else would he have a picture of it in a separate file?"

Penny tsked. "I bet he has this information for everyone in the folders. Let's read Marge's file."

When Allie opened the new file and Penny started to read, she put her hand over her mouth and aged in front of Jillian and Allie. Like Nancy's, the files contained Marge's banking information, identity cards, and signature sample. "Oh, land's sake." Penny's voice sounded faint. "I don't know what to say. I believed Stan was bad news, but I didn't expect this. I don't know how

I'll tell Marge."

Jillian covered Penny's hand with her own. "For now, maybe don't say anything. Just ask her to check her other account balances. Maybe you could make up something you heard at the beauty shop about a scam. If you focus on Stan, I don't think she'll believe you."

"Sad to say, I agree. I hope he didn't steal all her money." Penny sighed and grew visibly shorter as she sat at Jillian's kitchen table.

"I do, too," agreed Jillian, squeezing her hand. "I need to spend some time reviewing these files. You don't think the drive has any viruses?"

"Nope, not after the scan I ran," Allie said. "But let's see if there's anything else interesting."

A single, untitled folder remained, and when Allie opened it, the three women saw only one file. When Allie clicked it, the file had one line of data—a string of numbers.

"What is it?" Allie asked.

"I don't know. Something Stan wanted to keep hidden," Jillian said slowly. "Penny, try not to worry. We'll get to the bottom of this. For now, let me make us some tea. We need something more soothing than coffee."

Chapter Thirteen

What do you wear to the funeral of an ex-boyfriend?
A thief? A murder victim? The decision was even more
difficult when the person held all three roles. Usually,
Jillian avoided wearing black to a funeral. She liked
funerals to serve as celebrations of a person's life.
However, with Stan's shady past, black seemed
appropriate.

A simple sheath dress, plain black pumps, and a
string of pearls would do the trick. She put her blonde
hair in a loose bun and applied neutral eye shadow, light
blush, and a little mascara. She made no effort to set off
her green eyes with eyeliner. Too much makeup seemed
inappropriate.

When she reached into the jewelry drawer for her
pearls, she saw the dried corsage from her high school
junior prom all those years ago. The pink roses had
developed brown edges, and black, crisp leaves had lost
their dark green shine. She had kept the corsage in a
small, clear "to go" box, and her mind returned to the
spring day Stan gave it to her. He had been awkward and
charming while he tried to pin it on her ivory, strapless
dress. The memory caused unexpected tears to sting her
eyes, and she dabbed them carefully, trying to keep her
makeup from smudging.

What went so wrong in Stan's life that he chose

crime? She believed his behavior had led to his death, and she wanted to prove it. Even though his actions seemed unforgivable, Stan shouldn't have paid for it with his life. Maybe she would see something at the service that would give her some direction on how to find his killer. She left earlier than necessary, not wanting to arrive late.

When Jillian picked up Allie, the artist had opted for the same black motif, but she personalized it in her unique way. Wide-legged black pants accompanied an oversized black jacket. A white top, black earrings, and black platform loafers finished her outfit. She climbed into the truck and glanced at Jillian.

"Classy, always," her friend said approvingly.

"Well, I didn't know what to wear," Jillian said. "Black seemed appropriate. I love your sense of style, but I don't have the personality to pull it off."

"Thanks. Are you holding up okay?"

"Yes, I guess. I hate how Stan's life spun out of control." Before she could elaborate, they arrived at the church.

Gina had scheduled the service for ten, and the lot was already crowded when they arrived at nine-thirty. Overflow mourners also parked up and down the street so they could escape quickly and return to their everyday lives. Most people couldn't think about death for very long. Jillian pulled a little down the street and joined the line.

She and Allie walked toward the chapel without talking. Jillian's face was flushed from both the heat and stress. Her response to tension began with her face becoming damp. She knew that, eventually, sweat would start to run down her neck. She approached the small chapel with growing nausea.

Even worse, with its gray cement bricks and pitched shingle roof, the building didn't welcome visitors. No cross or stained glass offered any relief. Before becoming a church, the structure had held a free-standing store, but Jillian had never seen it. The conversion had occurred before her birth. Like many churches in Oklahoma, this one had no denominational affiliation. Instead, about ten years ago, the current minister named it Followers of the Lamb Chapel. Jillian assumed Gina didn't know her husband's background in the First Presbyterian Church of Magnolia Hill, not that she should. His parents divorced, and his dad had gone to parts unknown while his mother, Sarah, lived near her sister in California.

Jillian wondered if Sarah would attend the service. She had always liked Stan's mother, and the woman welcomed her into the home and treated her like family. Stan's father, Jerry, not so much. Once she was an adult, Jillian assumed that Jerry probably had other emotional commitments. No one in town expressed surprise when they split shortly after Stan left for college. Surely, Gina knew Stan's mother and had reached out to her.

As they walked into the chapel, Jillian tried to keep her heels from clicking on the concrete floor. The smell assaulted her immediately—a sickening scent of too many flowers mixed with a hint of dust, mildew, and floor polish. She swallowed hard and glanced at Allie. "Where do you want to sit?" whispered her friend.

Jillian motioned to the back on the right side of the aisle. She walked through the pew and sat in the farthest seat. From there, she could scan the crowd to see who attended and how they responded.

On the front row of the church sat the attractive blonde who had led Stan away in the coffee shop just a few days ago. Her position in the chapel confirmed Jillian's suspicion that she had met Gina. The young woman dressed more simply than the day Jillian had seen her, but her taste and the cost of the clothing still showed. She appeared exhausted and strained even under expertly applied makeup.

Gina stared at the bier in front of her. Jillian thought she must hate sitting in the front of the room with all those eyes on her back. But the young widow sat there bravely—straight, head up, with only an occasional wipe of her hand indicating her grief.

A single, poignant red rose sat on a pedestal. Of course, Stan would need a closed casket, but the service appeared more like a memorial than a funeral. When Jillian looked at the rose, she remembered the corsage she had seen that morning. When had Stan decided that stealing led to better results than working? What inside his personality had brought him to this point? Whatever drove him, he had paid a high price for it.

Her eyes left Gina and the rose, and she began to search for Stan's mother. Jillian couldn't be sure she would recognize her, but an older, tall woman sitting near the front, if not on the first row, should be easy to spot. However, no one fit that description. Did Sarah not want to come? Jillian couldn't imagine such a thing. Otherwise, did Gina not invite her, or did her health not let her attend? Odd. She could ask Penny about it later. The blow-dry caucus would know.

Jillian gave up on finding Sarah, and her gaze wandered to the numerous sprays and baskets. Stan appeared well-loved in Magnolia Hill, whether or not the adoration was earned. Another woman, Betty, walked almost the length of the chapel. Stan's assistant sat down directly behind Gina. Betty's black dress seemed washed out, almost blue, like it had been her funeral outfit for several years.

Betty's visible stress level surprised Jillian. Heartbroken might have been a better word. She sat slumped in the pew, her head down and shoulders quietly shaking. From time to time, she glanced from the rose to the woman sitting in front of her. Both images seemed to make her cry harder.

Jillian tapped Allie on the hand. Focusing on her program, Allie jumped and yelped a little, but no one seemed to pay any attention. Jillian gestured at Allie and then glanced several times at the front of the chapel, willing her friend to look forward.

Allie watched Betty for a few minutes and turned toward Jillian in surprise. She dug in her bag for a pen and wrote a note on the funeral program. "Betty seems awfully upset." Jillian nodded in agreement.

Betty hadn't grown up in Magnolia Hill and didn't go to high school with Jillian. She wasn't married and didn't date, although rumors said she had a serious relationship in college that ended badly.

Between growing up in Magnolia Hill and owning a business in town, Jillian knew most residents. Although she believed she only had a few close friends, she had hundreds of acquaintances.

Betty, on the other hand, stayed to herself. Her mother got a clerical job at the nearby university and moved to Magnolia Hill after Betty left her to attend the same institution. However, the woman soon suffered a debilitating stroke, forcing Betty to drop out and move in with her and act as her caregiver. Jillian suspected that disruption also somehow led to the breakup with her boyfriend. Although her mother had died many years ago, Betty stayed in Magnolia Hill, still living in the same house and rarely going out.

Betty disappeared from Jillian's sight when a large man in a blue suit sat at exactly the angle to block her view. She strained a little to see around him and ultimately gave up. Instead, she glanced around the rest of the chapel to see who else had arrived. She saw business owners, classmates, and a large group of men in suits, likely friends from his time in Dallas. One of them went up to Gina and touched her shoulder. She stood up and hugged him.

Then Jillian saw a tall man sitting opposite the chapel, almost directly across from her. He also scanned the crowd, but he appeared angry. Not sad. Angry like he wanted to fight with someone, but didn't know who to choose. Jillian got Allie's attention again and motioned toward the stranger.

She whispered, "Do you know him?"

Allie shook her head no. Jillian nodded back at her, not wanting to make much noise in the quiet room.

Then someone started playing a wheezy organ. Jillian glanced up to see the organist and one plump singer perched inside a small balcony. She slightly resembled a roosting pigeon, and Jillian tried not to giggle. Finally, a somewhat out-of-tune, desperately ponderous "Amazing Grace" led into the eulogy.

As Jillian listened to the plump, balding minister describe Stan's life in glowing tones, she saw Gina's shoulders stiffen, but she just stared straight ahead and sat incredibly still. She appeared to be doing everything she could to avoid falling apart.

Betty, however, appeared to feel no such limitation. The notable sound of her crying shocked Jillian. Betty seemed quiet, even mousy, whenever she interacted with her. And yet, here she was, wailing away at Stan's funeral.

Finally, the minister stopped talking, and after everyone stood for the closing hymn, the pigeon-like soloist warbled "In the Garden." When the congregation reached the refrain, a loud crash stopped everyone, even the organist. Then people started talking excitedly.

Jillian heard someone yell, "Call an ambulance!" She strained on her toes, trying to see. At last, the man in the blue suit moved slightly aside, and she had a clear view. Betty had fainted and lay on the chapel floor.

Chapter Fourteen

The service came to a crashing end, and Allie stared at Jillian. "Jeepers." They stayed out of the way of the paramedics treating Betty.

Even though she had regained consciousness, she appeared confused, likely the result of hitting her head on the gray stone floor. They could see her arms moving, but she lay on the ground until the paramedics arrived. They checked her vitals, carefully transferred her onto the gurney, and started an IV.

After the ambulance pulled away, Allie and Jillian walked outside. No one had left, and Gina stood in the middle of a large crowd that included the men Jillian hadn't recognized inside. "You know any of those guys?" she asked. Allie shook her head no.

Other Magnolia Hill residents surrounded her, also. Phyllis, the owner of Phyllis' Flowers, had an arm around Gina's shoulders. Beside her stood Beau, the owner of Button's and Beau's, an upscale boutique. The man who hugged Gina before the service stood close to her, awkwardly moving his arms like a fluttering bird. A dozen or so older women, all wearing church dresses, hose, and sensible pumps, came up to Gina with sad expressions and open arms. Jillian hated to see Nancy and Marge as part of the group. Penny, wearing a green pantsuit and sandals, appeared ten years younger than the rest of them when she walked up to her friend and hugged her. Allie's grandmother and Marge talked with their heads together, and Jillian continued to scan the crowd.

She noticed Will standing close to Phyllis. He was shaking his head in bewilderment, like many of the attendees. She snapped her head away so quickly that Allie glanced over to see what had happened.

"Oh, Will's here," she said.

Jillian mumbled an acknowledgment.

"Jilly, I like Will. What's this about?" She ran a clean hand through her hair, and Jillian thought it might be the first time she had seen her friend without extra paint.

She dropped her head. "It doesn't matter. Can I just not like someone?"

"Of course, but you never act like this. You like everyone at almost an exhausting level. Something had to happen."

Jillian sighed. "I don't want to have this conversation right now."

Allie studied her black platform shoe for a moment. "I won't make you talk about it, but I wish you would."

"Fine. If I tell you, can we drop it?"

Allie nodded, and Jillian saw her friend's blue eyes had clouded because of her harsh words. "I'm sorry. I'm not mad, but I don't understand why I have to justify not liking someone. Do you remember Amber?"

"Sure, I do. You guys were tight back in the day," Allie remembered. "Wait a minute. Didn't she date Will?"

"She did until the night of the senior prom," Jillian said with a snarl.

"I remember that now. He stood her up, didn't he?" Understanding slowly showed in Allie's eyes.

"Yes, he did. And he never offered any explanations. He ghosted her. He never picked her up that night. She sat in the living room all evening, not believing he wouldn't show. To make it worse, he didn't call her for days. She was worried he'd had an accident and was relieved and angry when she found out he was okay. She tried to call his parents, but they blew her off, too. I think she cried for an entire week. She thought he would propose after graduation, and he just dropped off the planet instead."

"How awful! Did he ever call her again?"

"About a week later, he phoned and offered a vague apology. He didn't say where he had gone. Amber hung up on him, and I don't think they ever talked again. It sounds dramatic, but I heard the conversation on her end. I spent almost that entire week at her house. After graduation, she wanted to get away from Will, so she started searching for work out of the area—anywhere but Magnolia Hill. She was so embarrassed and upset that she wanted to start over, including excluding me from her life. Eventually, she went to college, but I lost track of her. Will cost me our friendship, too."

"I can't believe I forgot that," Allie apologized. "I wasn't close to Amber, and I think she always thought I was odd. But I understand why his behavior made you angry. He doesn't seem like a guy who would have blown off his girlfriend. I wonder what happened?"

"I don't know. I avoid him."

"Well, I'm sorry you've been upset this long." Allie offered a hug, and Jillian's mind moved from the past to the scene around her.

"Nothing to do about it now, but I'll never like Will."

Jillian surveyed the people milling around, and she noticed the man from the back of the church standing away from the group, leaning against the chapel bricks. Even though he wore sunglasses, Jillian saw that he looked at Gina, then glanced away, not wanting to stare. Finally, his shoulders shrugged, and his head dropped. He turned and stalked down the street to a midrange white truck. When the engine roared to life, everyone jumped a little and glanced up. The angry man sped away.

Even though she was curious, Jillian needed to focus on how to pay respects to Gina. She had no idea how to approach the widow, and her mind ran through several scenarios.

"Sorry about Stan. You remember me, the one threatening him." She laughed a little to herself. Probably a bad idea to remind Gina of her threat.

"Sorry about Stan. Do you know he steals the life savings of sweet little old ladies?"

Probably also inappropriate. Finally, Jillian took a deep breath and walked up to Gina. *Go with simple.* "Gina, I'm very sorry for your loss."

Gina regarded her cautiously and offered a quick, although tight, smile. "Thank you, Jillian. Stan thought you were great and had a lot of respect for you."

Jillian had no idea what to say. Maybe Gina meant it, or perhaps she also wanted to appear polite. Either way, the planner felt less nauseous having negotiated the encounter smoothly. "You're very kind. I can't imagine what you're going through. If you need anything, don't hesitate to reach out."

Gina murmured something in reply. Jillian hoped she didn't take her up on that last offer, but she needed a graceful exit that let her walk back to Allie.

When Jillian returned, her friend put a hand on her back. "How did that go?"

"Remarkably well. Gina seemed friendlier than I expected, and she told me that Stan respected me."

"How weird! I mean, you deserve respect, but I don't know that you want it from Stan. Sheesh, you know what I mean."

Jillian nodded. "Yes, I do, and you're right. Her reaction was weird."

She considered Gina's comment and watched Kandace roll up to Stan's widow, hug her, and start talking. Kandace loved everyone, and her patrons loved her. Jillian couldn't imagine anyone vandalizing her shop, and yet it had happened.

"I wonder how well Kandace knows her," mused Jillian, again remembering Kandace's suspicions about Stan.

"*Babcia* always says Kandace 'never met a stranger.' "

"True enough. You know, Kandace's accusations against Stan surprised me. That's a long time to carry around anger."

Allie stared at her friend in shock. "What are you saying?"

Jillian thought about the question. What was she suggesting? "I don't know. Nothing, I guess. Kandace wouldn't hurt anyone."

"No, she wouldn't." Allie stiffened. "Don't even think that Kandace caused Stan's accident."

"I'm not. I'm just frustrated. Maybe I'll stop by the

cafe later and see when she can reopen. And if I happen to ask questions about Stan…" Jillian paused at her truck and shrugged. "Wanna come?"

The painter huffed as she sat down and leaned back in her seat. "I do not want to be part of you questioning our friend. I've got a lot to get done today. I didn't have time for this morning, but I had to come."

Jillian didn't want Allie to be angry with her. "It was easier walking in with you. Don't worry. No one could have a better friend than Kandace. I don't think she had anything to do with Stan's death." Jillian squeezed Allie's hand, started her truck, and pulled onto the street.

Allie's shoulders relaxed, letting the planner know she was forgiven. "Jillian, you need to let this go a little. The police will figure it out. I never intended to miss the memorial, and I got the bonus of watching Betty collapse. She seemed devastated—almost like she was the one who had lost her spouse."

Jillian hit the brakes for a light, stopping faster than usual. "What did you just say?"

"She seemed more upset than his wife." Allie stopped. "Oh, Jilly, you don't think…"

"Honestly, I don't know what to think other than you just made an interesting statement. Maybe Betty loved Stan."

Allie thought for a moment and asked, "Did you know Stan was married?"

"Not until Penny told us. I wonder if Betty knew?"

"If not, I bet she was super mad when she found out."

"Yeah," Jillian said, pulling up in front of Allie's condo. "Angry enough to kill someone?"

Chapter Fifteen

While she drove back to the office after dropping Allie off, Jillian realized she needed to talk to Officer Gayle about Stan. She should have already done it, and if she waited much longer, her friend would be rightfully upset with her.

She dialed Gayle's cell, and the officer quickly picked up.

"Hey, Jillian, what can I do for you?"

"Are you busy later this afternoon?"

Jillian heard the officer sigh on the other end of the phone, but she answered cheerfully. "I've got time if you need to see me. Why?"

"I need to talk to you about Stan. I don't want to make it a big deal at the station, but I've learned a few things I think you should know."

"I'm free after three."

"How about meeting at Peachy Pies about three thirty? It would be a great time for some dessert," she said hopefully.

"Sounds good," agreed Gayle. "I'll see you then."

Jillian spent the rest of the day reviewing client portfolios and placing a few trades. Apparently, the funeral wore everyone out because her phone never rang. After the market closed at three, she drove toward the rustic diner and saw the sign shaped like a giant plastic pie a few blocks before arriving. She pulled into the gravel parking lot and hopped out. No surprise, Gayle already sat at a booth. The young officer waved her over.

"I hope you don't mind—I already ordered a piece of pie and some coffee."

"No, you read my mind. What's the special today?"

"Peach," Gayle said with a laugh as the waitress walked up with a steaming cup and a massive, glistening slice.

"That looks amazing. Get me one of those, too, please," said Jillian.

"No problem," the blonde waitress said. Tall, with a thin, silver eyebrow ring, she sounded tired when she took the order. The faint bruise on her cheek made Jillian wonder what awaited her at home. She said nothing, however, and the waitress walked away, her white sneakers squeaking on the stained linoleum floor.

"Do you know her?" Jillian gestured toward the retreating waitress.

Gayle hunched a little over her pie. "I do. Yes, the bruise means what you think, but I can't get her to leave him or press charges. I try every time I eat here."

"That makes you a good police officer. You always want to help everyone."

Gayle glanced away for a second. "I know how hard it can be to leave a bad situation." Then she cleared her throat and focused on her coffee cup, obviously unwilling to discuss it further. "What did you want to tell me?"

Jillian swallowed hard. "I've discovered something about Stan that you need to know."

Gayle stopped stirring her coffee. "What?"

"I think he ran a fraud inside his financial firm." She

told Gayle about Stan's lack of registration, bizarre brokerage statements, and hesitation to fill clients' requests for funds.

"Wow! If you're right, Stan hurt a lot of people. What a lowlife," Gayle said.

"Yeah, and if somebody else found out what he did, they might want to kill him."

"That's a serious accusation," Gayle said slowly.

"Are the police sure the wreck was only an accident?"

"Nearly, but your information might change things." She laid her fork down and took a sip of coffee, appearing lost in thought.

"Why? Did you find anything strange?"

"Jillian, you know that Jeff won't want me to tell you anything. He can act like the stereotype of a small-town police officer in a bad novel, right down to his love of donuts. Don't tell him I said that."

Jillian laughed. "Don't worry. I won't."

The officer continued. "He likes to keep control of his investigations. He wouldn't tell me things if he didn't have to. He sure won't share anything with you."

"But you do know something," pressed Jillian. She paused when the strained waitress came back with another cup and slice. "Looks yummy." The waitress didn't offer a response, turning around and squeaking back to the kitchen.

Then Jillian fixed her gaze back on Gayle, who sighed.

"Stan didn't hit his brakes. No skid marks. Nothing."

"Could he have gotten distracted?"

"Yes, but he drove completely off the road without

noticing it. It's always stupid to do something else while driving, but that curve seems a strange place to drive distracted."

Jillian agreed. "Yeah, I always slow down. Did you find his cell phone?"

"No calls, texts, nothing right before he left the road."

"And the police still ruled it an accident?"

"Be fair, Jillian, we didn't have a reason to think otherwise. Now, I wonder."

"Did you find anything else?" Jillian asked, trying to choose a reasonable tone between cheery and overly curious. Images of the thumb drive burned a hole in her brain.

"We found a briefcase, papers, and, like I said, his phone…what you would expect. I'll review everything again."

Jillian almost said something about the drive, opened her mouth, and closed it again. She didn't want to get in trouble later, but she didn't know whether or not the police would pursue the information she had found. Jeff's anger at her actions might make him minimize the value of what he had missed. Instead, she changed the direction of the conversation. "Did you notice the guy at the funeral sitting in the back?"

"Do you mean Derry Klingman?"

"I thought I knew everyone in town, but I didn't recognize him." Jillian took a sip of her coffee. She glanced around, but no one paid attention to their conversation. A young couple tried to keep a toddler from escaping while two old cowboys sat talking, the vinyl booth seats beside them holding well-worn hats. No one seemed to be listening.

Gayle continued, "Derry moved back a few months ago. You know his mom, Vera, and Penny play bridge together."

"She might be another client of Stan's. And I wonder if Derry caught on to the scam. He seemed angry." Jillian watched the toddler try to climb over the back of the seat, only to be pulled down by his laughing dad.

"I noticed that. Unfortunately, Stan snuck by my radar, too." Gayle sighed. "I think he might have gotten money from my Gigi."

"Your grandmother?" Jillian paused mid-bite.

"Yes, she was one of Stan's clients. She called me crying when he died. She told me often that she loved doing business with a local boy who had made it big." She glanced away at something only she saw. "Sorry, Jilly, she didn't mean any disrespect to you."

"Don't worry about it. How long has she worked with him?"

"I don't know. Since right after he opened. Gigi went to some event he held and told me the next day that she had signed papers."

"Oh gosh, that makes me sick."

"Me, too. I should have checked things over." Gayle put her final bite of pie in her mouth and chewed slowly.

"Don't blame yourself. Stan's charm helped him get new clients. And if he ran a fraud, his words would need to melt butter." Jillian sighed and closed her eyes.

"I'll talk to Gigi again and see how much money she gave him. I hope it wasn't much. I'll also look back at Stan's file and see if I notice anything else, especially in the papers we found."

"Thanks, I appreciate it. Remember, you can check

Stan's regulatory history for proof he hadn't registered as a broker or advisor in Oklahoma."

"Will do. Thanks, Jillian. I'm glad you told me what you found out. But now, please stay out of it."

Jillian knew better than to argue. "Okay, I just thought the police ought to know."

The waitress brought them their tickets. "Have a nice day," she said in a voice that suggested she didn't care anything about their day. They got out of their booth and walked to the ancient cash register. Peachy Pies didn't take credit cards.

After they paid, Jillian watched Gayle walk to her car. She knew that by omitting the thumb drive, she had just lied to her friend. Even though she felt justified in taking it, she knew Jeff might disagree, and the exclusion would hurt Gayle. She felt guilty but not enough to call her back.

Somebody had killed Stan. She shuddered, realizing she probably knew the person or the family. Imagine Magnolia Hill housing a murderer!

Chapter Sixteen

After she left Peachy Pies, Jillian returned to her office for a meeting with an estate attorney and his client. The client wanted to bequeath his earthly possessions to his dog, Clyde, and the lawyer begged Jillian to help convince him to choose human beneficiaries. It took a couple of hours, but Jillian finally talked him into leaving money to charity, some great nieces and nephews, and a friend who already loved his dog. By the time the grateful client and relieved attorney left, Jillian had a massive headache. She couldn't wait to get home.

Back in the cool air conditioning of her living room, she took some aspirin and lay down on the couch with her head on the armrest. Edgar jumped on her chest and folded his front paws under his body. She stroked his silky fur and let her mind wander.

Stan had stolen money from many people in Magnolia Hill. Could any of them, or their angry family members, have tampered with the car?

Beyond that, Betty seemed to love Stan. Had he been seeing women other than Gina? She'd ask Kandace, who always seemed to have her finger on the gossip pulse. A jilted woman could lash out after learning about his infidelity.

Of course, Kandace also had her issues with Stan, even though Jillian believed her friend had done nothing wrong. Still, her opinions of Kandace might be jaded.

Tampering with Stan's car didn't seem like a crime of passion. Cold and calculating, it seemed likely to be the final chapter of his scam. She needed to find a way to lower the number of suspects since it seemed like everyone in town, except Penny, had been a victim of his fraud.

She wanted to start with Derry Klingman, the dry cleaner with the deadly expression at the funeral. However, Jillian waited. Even if the cleaners were still open this late in the afternoon, she wanted to talk to him when he hadn't had the stress of today. She would have to wait until tomorrow.

Even after her pie and coffee, Jillian's head ached, and her stomach growled. Stress and migraine headaches always made her want to eat. She put together a ham sandwich on rye with crisp lettuce, tomato, and Swiss cheese and placed it on a paper plate with some sour cream onion chips and a pickle. Then she brewed another pot of coffee.

Edgar jumped up on the chair beside her and begged for a treat. She knew he shouldn't have any—ham had too much salt—but he grabbed her hand with his paw and didn't let go until he pulled it over to his mouth. A spoiled cat owned her.

Both of her animals possessed advanced manipulation skills. Agatha also could nuzzle up and talk Jillian out of a cookie or rub against her until she pulled out the brush and smoothed her mane. She didn't mind. Edgar and Agatha brought her so much joy that she enjoyed indulging them.

After Jillian and her hungry cat finished their sandwich, she pulled out her laptop and organized her notes on the older man and his dog. She would take her black suit to the new cleaners the next day. She needed a good excuse to meet Derry.

****

Jillian woke the following morning before her alarm, anxious to talk to the dry cleaner. Disturbed from his sleep, Edgar meowed. She knew he hoped for some bacon, and he glared at her when she only downed a coffee and rye toast. After breakfast and a quick shower, she grabbed the black suit, a couple of shirts, and a pair of navy slacks. She headed toward the cleaners, guided by her phone's GPS. Once she arrived, she grabbed her laundry from the back seat and entered the store.

The fresh, clean laundry smell greeted her, as did the man behind the counter. Jillian almost didn't recognize him as the angry person she had seen yesterday.

"Got some cleaning today?" he asked. His crisp speech didn't have the customary Oklahoma twang. Jillian thought he must have been born somewhere else—she suspected the Midwest.

"I do. Please dry clean all of this. I don't want it to fade or shrink." She pushed her pile of clothes closer to his side of the counter. Glancing behind him at the maze of hangers and clothing, she wondered how he could keep it all organized.

"No problem, Ms…" he trailed off.

"Jillian Bradford," she said. "And your name is…"

"Derry Klingman."

Jillian feigned surprise. "Nice to meet you finally, Derry. You come highly recommended. I think we have some friends in common."

The owner blushed. "Oh really? Who recommended me?"

"Penny Krol, Marge Fields, and more of their friends."

Derry smiled at the list of names. "I know all of them. My mom plays bridge with that group."

"I love Penny so much she's practically my own family," Jillian said.

"She's a firecracker, all right. My mom loves her."

"I do, too. I'm always amazed at her resourcefulness and independence. You know, she does most of her home repairs and invests her own money." Jillian waited to see his response.

Derry's pleasant demeanor melted, and she saw a flash of the angry man at the funeral.

"I wish she'd convinced my mom to do that."

Jillian decided to push a little more. "Well, Penny tells me that her friends tried to convince her to use Stan Savage, but she always had a funny feeling about him. And now that he's dead, they don't know what they'll do."

"They're probably better off, assuming they have any money left."

Bingo. Jillian decided to play stupid. She furrowed her brow. "What do you mean?"

"Well, Mom always told me that Stan was amazing and made a lot of money in her portfolio. I finally reviewed her statement, and it didn't look anything like my portfolio statements. I don't believe he invested any of her money. I'm afraid he spent it." With his anger, his speech became even more staccato than earlier.

"What did you do?"

Derry leaned forward, his arms on the counter beside Jillian's stack of clothing. "I went to talk to him the day he died. Bad timing on my part." He sighed and then continued. "Anyway, I asked him about his investment strategy for Mom's money, and he tried to use some financial words on me. He didn't realize I had a business degree, and I knew all those terms. But I'd never heard them strung together that way. He didn't make any sense, and I told him so."

"What did he say?"

"He seemed nervous, and he tried to hide it with arrogance. He said I didn't understand. Said he was a 'trained professional.' " Derry made air quotes and continued.

"I told him I understood plenty and that he'd better give my mother her money back. He told me he would, but I guess I got pretty loud. His assistant came into the office to see what was happening, but Stan motioned her back out again. I left and sat in my Toyota for a long time, trying to decide what to do. He finally came out and got in his fancy yellow Porsche."

"Did he see you?"

"I don't think so. I decided having another fight outside wouldn't help, and all I wanted was for him to return Mom's money. I watched him drive off, I guess right before his accident, and now I don't know what to do." He took the pressure off his arms, marked with deep creases from the counter, and stood up straight. Derry's eyes were bright, and he blinked a couple of times. Jillian felt sympathy for his stress.

"Have you talked to the police?" she asked.

"And tell them I got in a screaming match with a guy who drove off the road a couple of hours later? No thanks, and I hope you don't tell them either." He glared at Jillian darkly for a minute, resembling the man the day before, before he forced a strained smile back on his face.

Jillian plastered one on, too. "No, I won't say anything. But I think you should consider it. Anyhow, when can you have my laundry ready to pick up?" This conversation needed to come to an end. Derry picked up the stack of clothes.

"How about tomorrow afternoon?" he said flatly.

"Great," she said. "I'll see you then." She walked quickly out of the store, glad to leave. She glanced around and saw that the only car in the lot was a black Toyota. She jotted down the tag number on an envelope before she drove away.

Chapter Seventeen

After Jillian had dropped off her laundry, she checked her watch. She still had three hours before her next client meeting—plenty of time to check on Kandace.

She walked into the coffee shop, smelling the fresh paint before she saw the clean walls. Boxes of new ceramicware sat on the counter, and the tables and chairs were arranged in their usual places.

Kandace rolled up. "Hey, Jilly, what a crazy few days."

"Tell me about it. How are things here?"

"Almost back to normal if you don't count the 'Bytes' part of my name. I don't have computers, and I'm still waiting on a new refrigerator, so I can't make you a sandwich or snack."

"I didn't come here for food. I wanted to check on you." She didn't want to think about her desire to pump her friend for information.

"You're sweet," Kandace said, and Jillian felt guilty. "But I can offer you regular coffee if you'd like it."

"You know me. Thanks, I'd love it."

"No trouble at all."

Jillian watched Kandace working behind the counter, ashamed that she even considered that she would hurt Stan. Kandace had always been remarkable. In high school, she ran track and won state competitions every year. She expected to go to college on a scholarship.

Then the hit-and-run drunk driver left her almost completely paralyzed from the waist down. She could stand a little but spent most of her life now in her customized wheelchair.

Jillian had watched Kandace struggle over the years as she learned new ways to do everything. But her spirited friend decided she would not let the accident define her, and it didn't.

The space had been empty for almost a year when she opened the coffee shop with part of her insurance money. Previously, a nondescript restaurant pitifully named "Food" offered an environment of cheap, plastic booths and average fare.

When Food finally closed, Kandace purchased the space and remodeled it in shiny metallics with gunmetal walls. The floor gleamed with polished gray tiles also placed to create accent squares on the walls. Comfortable, chrome chairs upholstered with black flecked fabric established spaces easy to occupy.

The laptop computer connections and southwest-style tapas provided "bytes" and "bites." Most importantly, Kandace's coffee was famous for its quality. Whipped drinks with fancy names were plentiful and delicious, but the coffee bar featured an expansive menu of beans, ground to order and French pressed. The shop was popular with adults and students, and Jillian still couldn't imagine why kids would randomly vandalize Kandace's hard work. More than that, when she thought about her friend's accomplishments, she realized she would never throw it all away out of revenge. Kandace might know something helpful, but she hadn't been involved in Stan's accident.

She set her thoughts aside when Kandace rolled back with a large cardboard cup filled with fragrant, steaming coffee. "Are you doing okay, Jillian? You must have had a rough few days, too."

"The week has been tough. Old memories keep surprising me. I cared about Stan in high school, but his arrogance got worse every year. I've always believed the pressure from his dad caused some of that." Jillian glanced many years in the past, but quickly she returned her gaze to Kandace, sensitive to her friend's concerns about Stan. "How are you?"

"The destruction spooked me," Kandace admitted, gesturing around the room. "On top of that, whenever I see a bad car accident, I have PTSD."

"I can't even imagine," Jillian said quietly. "We can change the subject."

"No, it's a relief, to be honest. I hate to bring up old events to my friends."

"You can talk to me anytime you want. I won't pretend to understand, but I'll listen." Her eyes filled with tears, brought about by exhaustion, sadness, stress, anger, and guilt that she doubted her friend. She bent down and hugged Kandace.

The barista brushed her eyes but straightened up in her chair. "What else can I get you, Jilly?"

"You hear all the good gossip. I don't understand how Stan's car lost control. I wonder if anybody said anything to you."

Kandace shook her head. "No, they haven't. I don't understand it, either. He seems to have lost control, alone, on a sunny afternoon. Weird. If I hear anything, I'll let you know." She stared off for a while and then sighed. "In other news, Betty's performance at the memorial was worth an Academy Award."

"I don't know. It seemed a little overly dramatic to me," laughed Jillian.

Kandace continued, "For Gina's sake, I hated how the service ended so abruptly and disrespectfully. I can't imagine her stress level, and then the focus turned to someone other than her. Betty wasn't being fair, and Gina deserved everyone's sympathy that day."

"Do you know Stan's wife well?" Jillian was relieved that her friend brought up the subject.

"I wouldn't call us close, but I've talked to her several times. I think she started staying with Stan recently because she only started coming to the shop a few weeks ago. She mostly came with him, but sometimes she dropped in alone."

"What's she like?"

"Gina's all right. Of course, she wears more designer clothes than I do—actually, more than most of my customers. But she always takes the time to talk. She's not as extra as she appears."

"That surprises me," admitted Jillian. "I guess I shouldn't judge a book by its cover or a woman by her manicure."

Kandace laughed. "She doesn't get manicures. I noticed her polish perfectly matched her outfit the other day. She told me she does her nails so that she can keep them coordinated with her clothes."

"Seriously? I figured her for a manicure girl. You notice the details!" Jillian said with respect.

Kandace nodded, but then her face turned somber.

"I feel awful for her now."

"I do, too. Does she have a job?"

"She's an accountant. Her clients primarily live in Tulsa, but technology let her change her interactions. She realized she could do most of her work and meetings remotely, and her clients didn't care, so she came to Magnolia Hill to spend more time with Stan."

Jillian nodded. "I didn't know that he had a wife."

"I didn't either until she started coming in. The first time Stan introduced her, of course, I tried not to look surprised. I didn't think Stan was the marrying kind."

"Not at all. I thought I had seen him with different women."

"You might have," Kandace confided. "I saw him with several women here. They didn't seem like business meetings."

"Did you ever see him with Betty?"

Kandace was suddenly intent on her cup of coffee. "I shouldn't say anything 'cause it's none of my business. But yes, I saw him with Betty several times."

"And you don't think you saw a business meeting they decided to have here? Katherine and I have working lunches all the time," Jillian pressed.

"No, not from their behavior, especially Betty's laughing. She seemed much more cheerful than average. Of course, she's always depressed. And then, yesterday at the memorial…" Kandace's voice trailed off. "I don't think she was faking it."

"Do you think Gina knows?"

"I hope not. I didn't want to say anything to make a complicated situation worse. But if she stays here even a little longer, someone will tell her about Stan and his other women."

"How many did you see him with?" Jillian asked.

"I don't want to gossip. Honestly, I don't know. A lot."

"He brought in women other than Betty?"

"Jillian, Stan brought at least half a dozen different women here."

"In front of you?" Jillian said incredulously. "Boy, he had a lot of nerve."

"Yeah," Kandace agreed. "Like I was just another accessory of the coffeehouse, a cup or plate. I told you earlier that Stan wasn't my favorite person. Even though he's dead, my opinion of him hasn't changed."

Jillian again pushed aside the thought that Kandace might have hated Stan more than she wanted to admit. Still, it would have resulted in her giving him a cussing, not tampering with his car. She refocused on Gina and Betty, two people she cared about far less. "Gina could have figured out his infidelities. Betty could, too."

"I guess so, especially Betty because she lives here."

Jillian took another deep drink of the delicious coffee. "I sure would like to talk to her."

"Let me know what you find out!"

"I will. Hey, can I ask you one more question? I don't think you're going to like it."

Kandace quirked an eyebrow.

"Are you sure your vandalism was only random?" Jillian asked.

Her friend paled a little and rolled her chair back. "Are you asking if I think someone deliberately destroyed my coffeehouse?"

Jillian said nothing and just held her gaze.

"I hope not," Kandace finally said. "Why would someone want to target my shop or me? I haven't done anything to make someone mad." She slowly rolled back and forth.

"I know you haven't. But I have trouble believing the vandalism randomly happened the same night that Stan wrecked."

"But, Jillian, that means you think someone tampered with Stan's car, too."

"Maybe." Jillian tried to hedge.

"Wow, that's a lot to process."

"Go with me for a minute," Jillian said. "Let's assume someone vandalized your shop for a reason. I've spent the last few days trying to think of something, and all I can come up with are your computers."

"My computers?"

"Could someone have used your internet cafe to contact another person without getting caught? Maybe Stan or one of his girlfriends wanted to contact each other on the down-low. Or maybe someone else looked up information about Stan and didn't want to be discovered."

"Information?" The uncharacteristic quiet of the coffeehouse caused the question to ring through the room.

Kandace's question reminded Jillian that her friend didn't know about the fraud.

"I think he had some funny business practices. The way he opened accounts and provided client information seems odd, but maybe people didn't understand," Jillian blurted out, feeling her face flush. She was a terrible liar, especially to her friends. "I wondered if you could access your computers' browser histories."

Kandace shook her head. "No, I can't do that. My patrons count on keeping their privacy. I do have sign-in sheets of the people who use the computers, though."

"Were they damaged in the break-in?"

"I keep the completed ones in my safe in case I ever need them for legal reasons. The night of the break-in, I only lost about half a completed page of names with blank sheets underneath. The vandals stole the whole stack."

"Did they empty every drawer here?" Jillian asked.

"No, they tore up a few, but the rest stayed unopened. I figure somebody or something scared them off."

"That's lucky. Could I see the list of the people who used your computers?"

"I can do that. It just sat on the counter by the register. Anyone could look at it."

"Great. I'll come back later and make copies of them when I have more time."

"I'll put them aside for you."

"The shop's fixed up good as new, and I appreciate the unofficial coffee."

"Thanks. I'm ready for all this to be finished."

Jillian hugged her friend, left the chilly coffee shop, and stepped into the bright heat. First, she'd lied to Gayle about the thumb drive, and now she had lied to Kandace about the fraud. Two lies to two friends in two days. She felt like a jerk, but she wanted to know more before she said much. Had the vandalism been random? Did Betty, Gina, or anyone else learn about the others? Had someone hated Stan for his fraud? Jillian had no idea how the pieces fit together.

Chapter Eighteen

The following morning, Jillian woke early to soft light and singing birds. Without showers, the afternoon might be less oppressive. Oklahoma always needed rain in the summer, but the daily rain was ridiculous. The wet weather pattern also needed to break before the 4th of July parade.

She took her phone off the charger and checked her schedule. With no meetings until midafternoon, she decided to review her emails, make some calls, and then reach out to Betty before she left for work. Two hours, three client calls, and a pot of coffee later, Betty answered the Savage Financial number on the third ring.

"How do you feel after your fall?" Jillian asked. Edgar rubbed his face against her cell phone and ignored her gentle dismissal.

"Embarrassed. Sad. Hurt. I know the correct answer is 'fine.' I mean, I'm okay physically. But, you know…" she trailed off. "Sorry. I'm fine," she finished stiffly.

"You don't have to say that. Can I drop by the office later today?" Edgar rubbed harder, and Jillian got up and gave him a treat out of the horse trailer cookie jar. Happily crunching, he finally left her alone.

Betty's voice developed a noticeable chill. "Why? What do you want to talk about?"

"I wanted to talk about Stan for a minute. I know

how hard all this must be. Are you going to have lunch?"

"Of course," Betty said. "But I don't want to answer a lot of questions over a meal with you."

"I understand." Jillian ignored the dig. "Feel like a hamburger? We could go to Burger Bonanza. My treat," she pressed.

"You're not going to take no for an answer. Okay. Fine. I'll meet you there."

Burger Bonanza had opened recently in a newer section of Magnolia Hill. A local car dealership owner had grown tired of pushing the latest models. He wanted a change, so he opened the restaurant.

Now that he owned a popular lunch spot, his focus had changed, but the shtick remained. He sold burgers like he sold cars. His loud, some called obnoxious, ads now peddled burgers instead of vehicles. In them, he always wore plaid suits and frequently employed gimmicks like rubber chickens and sound effects. Even the new Burger Bonanza sign had a gaudy plaid background. Still, they were the best hamburgers in town with onion rings like nowhere else. Jillian didn't know where he had found his cook, but that person deserved a raise.

When she walked under the plaid sign and entered the restaurant, all the waitstaff yelled, "Welcome to Burger Bonanza!" Those poor people deserved a raise, too. But today, the noisy atmosphere suited Jillian's mood. She didn't want anyone to overhear her, and the deafening lunch rush guaranteed privacy.

She saw Betty sitting off to the side in a booth with high sides. She wore a gray shirtwaist dress, white cardigan, and no makeup. Unlike Gina, the admin looked nothing like Stan's type, but Jillian put aside her catty thoughts and walked up to her with a bright smile. "Betty, how are you doing?"

Betty just shrugged. "I already ordered. You probably ought to do that, too, before we get started. I don't have much time. I have to get back to the office."

After Jillian ordered a bacon cheeseburger and the dreamy onion rings at the counter, she sat back down across the table from her. "I bet the office phone is ringing off the hook. How's everything?"

"I'd rather not say."

"Okay." This was going well, thought Jillian, so she decided to jump right in. "Betty, how much did Stan tell you about the business?"

"What do you mean?" Betty's eyes flashed defiantly, and the mousy secretary put up her guard.

What made Betty so defensive? Maybe she believed Jillian was suggesting she didn't work, and Jillian dialed back her words a little. "I don't know, just day-to-day stuff. Like how did you open new accounts? Did you help him with that?"

"No," Betty said. "Stan did all that when he met the clients."

Jillian didn't know if she was relieved or worried that Betty's story tied to Nancy's. "Did you help him with any of the paperwork?" Katherine handled everything like that in their office.

"No, Stan said he could take care of that himself."

The burgers came, and Betty seemed relieved at the distraction. After Jillian had consumed a few bites of burger and a couple of the golden, crispy onion rings, she continued trying to figure out what Betty did for Stan.

"If you don't do the paperwork, what did you do to help Stan with his business?" She winced, sure that Betty would take offense at her question, but surprisingly, she didn't.

"Mostly, I answered the phone and kept his calendar. At the end of each day, Stan would give me his schedule for the next couple of days, and I'd write it down. That way, if someone called, I'd know when he was busy."

"You only talked to Stan's clients when they called the office?" Jillian was still amazed, thinking about how Katherine knew their clients as well as she did.

"Right," she said. "I don't know why everybody keeps asking me. That's what I told them."

Jillian perked up. "Told who?"

Betty glared, and Jillian noticed a small amount of mustard stained the side of her mouth. She wiped her own face with a napkin, just in case. "I don't want to talk about it," Betty said flatly.

Frustrated, Jillian decided to change tactics. "Of course, you don't have to, Betty. Did you hit your head when you fell?"

Betty rubbed her frizzy hair. "Yeah, but not that hard. Or else I've got a hard head." Jillian welcomed the first glimpse of a smile forming at the corners of her mouth.

"I've been accused of the same thing," she said.

"I probably shouldn't have gone to the service. I certainly should have sat in the back."

"Well, funerals are always stressful." Jillian chose her following sentence cautiously. "Especially if you care about the person."

Tears started rolling down Betty's cheeks, and Jillian knew her suspicions about Betty's feelings were right.

"Yeah," she said.

"I'm sorry," Jillian said, and Betty's tears flowed faster.

"Yeah, me too. I never expected…"

"For Stan to die?"

"I wasn't going to say that." Her voice grew cold again, and Jillian quit talking for a second and took another bite of burger, trying to decide how to continue.

She took a risk and forged ahead. "What did Stan do after he graduated and left Magnolia Hill?"

Betty looked up in surprise, not seeming to expect that question. "He never talked a lot about it. I know he had trouble finding a job after graduating from college. He wanted to start at the top, not work his way up." Jillian noticed it was the closest Betty had come to being critical, but she didn't say anything, and the woman continued. "Stan complained that people didn't want to pay him what he thought he was worth. Eventually, though, he went to work for a financial services company."

"Do you remember the name of the firm?" She had to speak loudly over the din of the patrons and the exuberant welcome they all received.

"Oh, let me think. No, I don't remember. Maybe three last names? I didn't pay that much attention to the name of his old firm. What's this about?"

Jillian ignored her question, suspecting she wouldn't get another opportunity to fill in some gaps. "In Dallas?"

"I think."

"Do you know why he left and came back to Oklahoma?"

"I guess he didn't like the job. I don't know why."

114

Betty drew herself up and leaned back from the table. "Listen, Jillian. I told you I didn't want to answer a bunch of questions."

Jillian stopped talking to finish her onion rings. She wiped the last one in the remaining catsup before popping it in her mouth. So good!

Jillian looked sadly at the empty plate, then she focused again on the conversation. Betty either didn't seem to know much about Stan, or she wasn't willing to share what he told her. "I'm not trying to pressure you, but Stan's behavior doesn't make sense. Do you know how long he lived in Oklahoma before coming back to Magnolia Hill?"

"I never asked." Betty pushed her plate away with half her burger uneaten.

Jillian wanted to scream. How could Betty be in love with a man she didn't know? She tried a different direction. "When did he meet Gina?"

A dam broke, and tears and words flooded out. "I didn't know anything about a wife. He never told me about her. Would I have dated him if I knew he was married? The police also want to talk to me about Gina, but I don't know anything, Jillian."

"The police?"

"See," Betty accused, "you got me so upset I told you. Please don't mention it to anyone else. The police want to talk to me about Gina."

Jillian just nodded. She wasn't surprised Jeff and Gayle wanted to ask Betty some questions. Discovering that your boyfriend's married might be enough motivation to kill him. On the other hand, the police might only want to talk to Betty about Stan's business. Either way, Jillian wouldn't want to face Betty's upcoming afternoon.

"I know you were driving his car around noon, but what were you doing the night Stan died?"

Betty raised her eyebrows for a second, but she quickly recovered. "I never drive Stan's car," the woman said sullenly. "I don't have to tell you anything."

"Of course, you don't," Jillian assured. "But you might consider telling the police the truth."

The assistant's brief attempt at bravado crumbled. "Please don't tell anyone you saw me. Sometimes, Stan lets," she corrected herself, "let me drive his car when I'd run errands for him."

Jillian's eyes narrowed. "What errand would take you by the barn?"

"Stan loved the pulled pork sandwiches at Billy's BBQ. After I picked up the mail, I got one for him."

"If you're telling the truth, why were you so angry driving a fabulous car on a sunny day?"

"Because I wanted to run errands on my lunch hour, and I didn't have enough time." Betty sounded panicked. "I didn't want to kill him over it. I was annoyed, not murderous."

Jillian didn't know whether or not to believe her. She couldn't help but picture lonely stretches of road where a jilted Betty could pull onto a gravel drive, tamper with the car, and return to the office with a sandwich. To keep herself safe, she must have only loosened or punctured something, not broken it altogether. Still, Grady hadn't noticed anything.

She'd have to consider methods later. Now, she needed to keep Betty's confidence, so she'd talk. "I hate it when my plans go south," she agreed. "I still think you should tell the police because I may not be the only one who saw you. Did you talk to anyone later in the afternoon?"

"After I got back to his office with lunch, I made a couple of phone calls. Then I went to the farmer's market over in Big Sky. They stay open one evening a week. I don't know your game, Jillian, but I've got to get back to the office. Thanks for lunch, but leave me alone now." Betty picked up her white purse with worn, rough corners and shook Jillian's hand.

"I'm sure someone saw you," Jillian said more confidently than she felt. Big Sky was a couple of towns over. Unless she had friends there, most people wouldn't recognize Betty. Rural Oklahoma also didn't have surveillance cameras everywhere. Betty might have trouble getting an alibi.

After she paid the waitress, she tried to assure Betty some more. "It will all turn out okay. Just tell the police the truth."

"At this point, I don't even know the truth," Betty said sadly.

Chapter Nineteen

After lunch, Jillian went back to her office. She picked up the day's scattered mail, pushed through the door slot, and checked the phone messages, jotting notes about a client who needed money and a prospect who wondered if she could schedule an appointment. She ignored the call telling her she had won a million dollars and considered again investing in a system where her phone would ring anywhere. However, Katherine would return to her front desk soon, and Jillian didn't want every advertising call going to her phone.

She started working in her quiet office and jumped when the laptop's phone app rang. Her dad's number popped up, requesting a video call, and Jillian pressed the "Accept" button.

Suddenly, her parents' faces appeared on her screen, and Jillian began waving, laughing at herself. Why did everyone wave at a camera? She saw her parents waving back and laughing, and then their audio opened.

"Jilly! Hi, sweetie! How have you been?"

She grinned at their images. She knew she looked a lot like her mother, but her mom's wavier hair had streaks of gray. Her dad sat at least six inches higher than her mom, and his dark hair was gray at the temples. Although both sixty, they acted younger than some of her friends.

"Mom, Dad, where are you?"

"Still tramping around the English countryside studying stone circles," her father said. "The last couple of days, we've visited Castlerigg, and the Helvellyn mountains are breathtaking."

"Sounds fabulous," Jillian said. "I'll have to go someday."

"Any time you're free, you're welcome," her dad said. "I can always use another assistant!"

"How's your world, sweetie?" her mother asked again.

Jillian paused for a minute, not wanting to worry her folks, but she needed to talk to them about Stan. They always gave good advice, and she admired how they played off each other's ideas.

She told the stories of Stan's con and accident, and her mom paled enough to show through the bad video streaming over the laptop. Apparently, their B&B in Castlerigg had sketchy Wi-Fi.

"Jillian, we're so sorry. Your dad and I never cared for Stan, but we knew you did. He just came off a little too smooth for our taste, but we thought the best approach was to let you work it out yourself. We always believe in you."

Jillian's eyes prickled with tears. She loved her parents so much. "I know. I hope we can find the money, so half the town hasn't lost their savings."

"I do, too, sweetheart," her dad said. The lines in his forehead drew together between his eyes. "Please stay out of it and be careful. I know you like mysteries, but this situation sounds dangerous."

"You're right." Jillian sighed. "I think I like fictional murders more than real ones. I'll be careful."

"We know you will. Just wish we were a little closer right now to support you," he said. "Give our love to Allie and Penny. I hate to cut this short, but we have dinner reservations. We wanted to call you before it got too late."

"I'm glad you're having a blast. What's for dinner?"

"A little restaurant in town focuses on upscale farm-to-table. We wanted to give it a try."

"Sounds yummy. Have a local specialty, and give me a full report. Love you."

"Love you, Jilly," chimed in her mother.

"To the moon and back," her dad said, waving again. "Bye."

Their picture disappeared from her laptop, and she paused for a minute before returning to work. The room seemed quiet after her parents' infectious laughter, and she missed them immediately. However, she had a project to finish before she could go home.

She opened her spreadsheet program and began to organize a document comparing small business retirement plans for a client who wanted to start something for his company. She pulled out a tax book to check the year's contribution limits. Although she didn't prepare tax returns, keeping up with the tax components of retirement planning was part of her job as a financial planner, and her clients enjoyed data that compared their options. She relished the work, and it made her sick to think about what Stan had done to the older citizens of Magnolia Hill. Her mind left her project and went back to the mystery.

If someone killed him, how had they caused an accident during the afternoon of a sunny day? She needed an expert to help her do some research—a real gearhead with a talent for technology and automobiles. Jillian knew Grady wouldn't want her to get involved, so she needed to find someone else. An image of Will leaning over the hood of a muscle car flashed through her head, but she immediately dismissed it. She would locate another mechanic before she asked him for help.

She turned her attention back to her job. Once she had finished the report for her client and confirmed the meeting for later that week, she got in her truck and called Allie.

Electric guitar and drums overwhelmed any hello. "Where are you?" Jillian screamed.

"Out at the midweek farmer's market in Big Sky," Allie yelled. "Old Thyme Rock 'n' Roll is just a few stalls up. You know them. They sell herbs and play classic rock at their booth. They have a huge crowd tonight and are almost out of plants and cut herbs. Hang on a sec. I've got to get a little farther away."

Jillian could hear the background volume drop with each step Allie took. Finally, the music was silent.

"Can you hear me now?" Allie parroted the old television ad.

"I can. What takes you to the farmer's market?"

"I've got some consignment paintings at a booth, and I needed to buy some vegetables that came from the ground, not a processing plant."

"Good for you! I had an interesting lunch with Betty today." Jillian turned the volume up on her phone. Even without the guitars, she could barely hear Allie.

"Do tell. What did she know about Stan?"

"Frighteningly little. She didn't know anything about his practice or his marriage. She was freaking out because the police wanted to talk to her this afternoon."

"How could Betty run Stan's office if she knew nothing about the business?" Allie continued to yell over the noisy background bustle.

"I don't know." Jillian sighed. "I don't understand why she didn't find the situation odd. She also admitted she drove Stan's car the day of the accident."

"How did you get her to do that?"

"I told her I saw her flying by the ranch. Didn't I tell you?"

"No! I think that might be important," Allie said.

"It certainly gave her the opportunity to tamper with the car," Jillian agreed.

"If the police have started interviewing people about Stan's death, do you think they have the same list of names we found on the thumb drive?"

"Maybe. I hope they want to talk to Stan's family, friends, and clients. I know they interviewed Derry Klingman, the dry-cleaning guy who looked like he wanted to punch someone at the funeral. And now they've interviewed Betty, too. I guess Gayle believed me and talked Jeff or their supervisor into a further investigation."

"I would think learning about the fraud would make them suspicious." Allie's voice changed instantly from chatty to cautious. "Uh, Jillian…"

Jillian heard her but remained focused on Betty and interrupted. "Do you know anyone who could confirm if Betty went to the market the night Stan died?"

"Uh, Jillian," Allie said again more softly. "Listen to me. Betty's here right now."

"What?"

"I think she can't hear me over the band. She's standing by the batik T-shirts, and I'm on the produce side by the okra, but she keeps staring right at me."

"You're right. I don't think she could hear you, but you need to keep your guard up," Jillian said.

"Okay, I don't like creepy," Allie whispered. "I'm getting out of here."

Jillian heard Allie's quick footsteps and labored breath while she hurried with heavy bags of produce. Then she heard a car door slam, and the phone went silent until Allie spoke.

"Jeepers, Jillian, why was Betty watching me?"

"I don't know. She seemed freaked out at lunch today. Maybe she has a guilty conscience. I hope she didn't hear you."

As more and more road separated Betty and Allie, her voice sounded less strained. "I don't know how she could have heard anything over the music."

Jillian's breath still caught in her throat. "You don't see a car following, do you?"

"Nope, I keep checking my rearview mirror. Nobody's back there."

"Okay, keep your eyes open. I'm headed home now, so call me if you need anything."

Chapter Twenty

As Jillian pulled into her drive, she saw a large package on her front porch, brought it into the living room, and opened it. Edgar immediately hopped inside, crouching down so only black ears and shiny black eyes peeked over the top.

"Get out, kitty! You can't have both the box and the package." Edgar ignored her, pawing at the brown paper and plastic wrap. Flashes of red, white, and blue confirmed her suspicions that Agatha's new saddle pad had arrived. Agatha needed to exhibit some patriotic spirit, and the new tack would match Jillian's outfit.

With the saddle pad out of the plastic wrap, she left the box and brown paper for Edgar. He happily burrowed like she had bought it just for him. She laughed, his antics helping to relieve the pressure in her neck. She put a hand on each shoulder and stretched from side to side. Between her knowledge of Stan's scam and her belief that he had been murdered, her stress level was through the roof. Some barn time would help with that.

Before she left, she pulled out the last of the pasta salad from her fridge. Yes, the flavors blended over time, but she was pushing her luck with its freshness. She needed to finish it tonight, or she'd have to throw it out. She sat at her table, eating it from the container without even bothering to put it into a bowl. Edgar jumped up beside her and got a couple of pieces of ham. Satisfied, he bounced back onto the fireplace mantel and washed his face and whiskers.

Her impromptu meal finished, Jillian changed into jean shorts and a beachy tank top and laced up her boots. Then she grabbed her new saddle pad and jumped in her truck.

The sun remained higher than the barns, and the lush green grass divided by white metal fencing glistened in the early evening golden rays. Even the temperature had begun to moderate. It was still hot, but the Oklahoma wind no longer felt like it came from a microwave.

Jillian heard Agatha's greeting long before she got to the mare's run. She held up the red, white, and blue tack with its soft, cottony back.

"Hey, pretty girl, do you like your new saddle pad?"

Agatha sniffed it and nodded her head up and down, giving a short reply that sounded a little like a laugh. Jillian giggled.

"You're enthusiastic. I bet you want a snack!" Agatha responded again and pawed the ground while Jillian opened the treat lid and pulled out several apple cubes. She gave them to her one at a time so the exuberant horse wouldn't eat them all in one bite.

"Let's go play. We don't need to try this new pad, but we'll have fun. And I need fun right now." Agatha nodded again, so Jillian saddled her up and led her to the outdoor arena.

The yellow rays had changed to oranges and reds pouring across the western sky. Jillian mounted up, and they both enjoyed the evening for a minute. Then she clucked and led her off gently with her leg, and they walked around the arena. Jillian saw other owners coming out to clean and feed, and she offered cheerful waves to all of them. Other people might fuss and squabble with each other, but no barn drama for her. The ranch was her happy place.

They picked up the pace to a trot, which Jillian sat rather than posted. Then they loped a bit, but Jillian didn't want either of them breaking too much of a sweat. Whoever thought riding involved just sitting on a horse had never tried the sport.

After they stopped, she slid off and walked Agatha back to her run. She removed the new, slightly dusty tack and brushed both the horse and the pad. Agatha's coat was dry, so she gave her another treat and petted her forelock while she talked to her.

"How do I figure out who killed Stan? I'm sure he didn't just drive off the road."

Agatha stomped her foot, and Jillian noticed a horse fly on her ankle. She gave it a good shot of fly spray, and it fell to the ground. Agatha stomped her foot again, the sparkling polish Jillian painted on her hooves glittering red from the sun. Jillian laughed and rubbed her neck. "You know most horses don't like fly spray. I'm glad you're so easy."

She spritzed the horse one last time with citronella-smelling relief. "You're the best girl in the world. I'm sorry, I've got to go. I need to finish some work." Agatha picked up her foot, sighed, put it down, and dropped her head for one last pet.

****

The next day, Jillian didn't call Betty in advance. She just went to Stan's office. He had chosen to open Savage Financial in a newer part of Magnolia Hill. The building sat in a row of identical offices near a strip mall that featured the kinds of stores you see up and down the interstate. In Jillian's opinion, Stan's location was bland and joyless. She much preferred the quirky, antique arts district surrounding her office.

She pulled her truck up in front of Stan's sign. To the left, a red "For Rent" sign with a phone number filled the window. On the right side, a chiropractor had painted the image of a spine on her glass. Kingman's Cleaners sat only a couple of blocks away. Certainly, Derry worked close enough to drop by whenever he had a question.

Jillian opened the door, and an electronic chime announced her arrival. The large lobby still smelled faintly of new carpet. Betty sat on a basic office chair behind a Formica desk pushed into the corner. Her workstation mirrored the dullness of her clothing—a beige skirt and a white high-neck blouse, in spite of the heat, with loafers. Her mouse-brown hair was still unstyled and frizzy, even when she was at work. Worse, poor Betty was crying into a tissue.

"Oh, Jillian, I don't know what to do," she wailed, not even bothering to say hello. "The police think I killed Stan. I'm scared to death they'll come to arrest me at any minute." She raised her head, and Jillian saw Betty's minimal makeup had still created brown and black stains down her face.

"Why did you come in?" Jillian asked.

"Because I don't know where else to go. Clients call all day asking about how to get their money. I don't know where Stan kept the accounts. He never told me." She played with a white coffee cup, and Jillian saw brown mascara stains on her old-fashioned, paper desk calendar. Did anyone still use those?

"Betty, look at me." Jillian needed to win the woman's confidence, even if she didn't trust her. "I don't think you killed Stan."

"You don't? I promise, Jillian, I didn't do it."

"If you'd killed him, why would you stay in the office?"

"To find the money?" Betty's point didn't help her case. The disheveled assistant ran her hand through her hair, making it stand even more on end.

"Maybe," Jillian agreed. "But I don't think you'd do that. I believe you didn't kill Stan. Even if you did, if I'm trying to help you, you won't kill me, right?" She gave her a bright smile, but her corny joke fell flat.

Betty managed an uninspiring weak shrug. "Right." She sighed.

Jillian glanced at her sharply. Certainly, if she was accused of murder, she'd deny it forcefully unless she had done it, and even if she were guilty, she'd proclaim her innocence with more force than Betty was now. She ignored the sudden chill that traveled up her spine and pulled a chair to the desk. "Do you know someone who would want to hurt Stan?"

Jillian inventoried the woman as Betty twisted a tissue, even though she knew it was unfair under these circumstances. Nothing about Betty was glamorous, hair, clothing, or nails. She bit them down to the quick, and her cuticles bled. If Stan had made a move on Betty, Jillian was sure he only did it to help his con or throw suspicion off himself.

Finally, Betty spoke. "That might be a long list."

"Why?"

"Everyone's mad at him. The clients want to know where he kept their money, and a ton of women have been calling. I guess he dated a lot." Her voice rose to a shrill level by the end of the sentence.

Jillian nodded sympathetically. "I hate to tell you, but I asked Kandace, and she admitted she saw him with other women."

Betty's eyes filled back up with tears. "Do we have to talk about my love life? It's bad enough that I've had to deal with Gina the last few days. She acts like she cares about me, always asking about my life, friends, and what I like, but I don't want a new friend. Did you know she didn't even bother to invite Stan's mother to his funeral?" She bit out the words.

"How do you know that?" Jillian asked in surprise.

Betty glared across the desk at her. "She told me. Of course, she claimed she tried to call the only number she could find, but if you want my opinion, she didn't try hard enough."

Jillian could understand Betty's anger, but maybe Stan and his mother drifted apart over the years. She also didn't want Betty to fall down the rabbit hole of focusing on Gina. "That's too bad. I wonder what happened." She paused for a second. "I wanted to talk to you more about Stan's business practices."

Betty pulled herself up from behind her computer. "I already answered your questions at lunch yesterday. I told you I don't know much about Savage Financial," she said defiantly.

Jillian glanced around Betty's workspace. Unlike Katherine's perpetual papers that she organized only at the end of each day, Betty's office appeared pristinely clean—no documents, no files, nothing. Other than a couple of pictures of a cat, the only items on the desk were the laptop and calendar. "Right. I just thought you might have remembered something."

"From yesterday?" Betty asked with disbelief. "Why do you care, Jillian? I know Stan took some of your clients, but you don't seem like the kind of person to hold a grudge."

Jillian paused. She still didn't know if Betty manufactured the tears for sympathy. She needed to proceed carefully. "You're right. I don't do things like that. But I can't figure out how Stan ran his business."

"Well, if you want to try to learn something, do you think you could help me at the same time?"

"I'll do what I can. What do you need?" Jillian asked cautiously.

"I don't know anything about Stan's paperwork. Would you help me go through his office and see if you can find the accounts? I just want to give up."

Jillian tried not to appear too excited. Of course, Betty might want an alibi, but going through Stan's files provided Jillian's best hope of figuring out his activities.

"Betty, of course, I'll help. Where would you like to start?" She put her arm around the uncertain woman, and they walked from the lobby into Stan's office.

Chapter Twenty-One

Betty opened the door to Stan's office, and she and Jillian stepped inside. The room was silent, and a coffee cup from Cancun, still a quarter full of scummy coffee, felt frozen in time. When the door closed behind them, both women jumped. Betty flipped on a light, and some of the gloom faded. In any other situation, it would have been a beautiful room. A large desk with a burled wood top faced the door. Jillian couldn't help herself. She ran her fingers over the swirls and grooves, feeling the smoothness. "What a gorgeous desk."

"Isn't it pretty? Stan said he bought it a few years ago, and he loves—loved—it." She changed the verb tense, and her tears started again.

A set of golf clubs sat propped in the corner of the office, and signed golf prints decorated the walls. Jillian wandered around, studying the memorabilia. "Stan must have been quite the golfer."

"He said that golf held the secret of life."

"That seems dramatic. Did he tell you what it was?"

"No, but I always thought it involved the fresh air, walking, and satisfaction of hitting a good shot."

"Spoken like a golfer," Jillian said.

"Nah, I'm just a hack," Betty protested. "Stan played more than I do."

Stan's presence, and maybe a hint of his cologne,

hung in the air, as Jillian went back to his desk. "Let's try to find anything that would give you something to tell clients so we can get out of here. It seems disrespectful to disturb the room very much."

"Okay, I'll check the file cabinet. You check the desk drawers."

Jillian opened the bottom drawer and found it empty besides a comb, razor, some antacids, a can of shaving cream, and the cologne she smelled. She had seen ads for the men's fragrance on television. She never understood what horses rising from the ocean had to do with cologne. Did Poseidon, the God of the Sea, really smell that good?

The second drawer held yellow legal pads of paper and bulk pens printed with "Savage Financial" and the website. Jillian slipped one of them into her pocket and kept going.

The top drawer had a partially filled notebook. Jillian studied the pages, but they didn't resemble any client notes she had ever taken. Random words—like the scribblings on a desk calendar—filled many pages. However, at least half the written sheets had two letters followed by a date and a dollar amount, varying from large values to small. Although the entries were odd, the volume of pages caught Jillian's attention. If the lines corresponded to client accounts, Stan really had taken advantage of everyone in town.

The sound of opening and closing drawers interrupted her, and she called out. "Have you found anything interesting in the cabinet?"

"Nothing in the bottom drawer—just some old magazines. But in other drawers, some notebooks look more like bank entries."

Jillian held up the notebook from the desk. "Like these?"

Betty stuck her head through the open door. "Yes, just like that. What are they?"

"I don't know," Jillian admitted.

"I also found a list of people I think live around here," Betty volunteered.

"So, you recognize some of them?"

Betty sighed, and her voice sounded sharp when she answered. "You know I've lived here for years. Just because I wasn't born here…" She trailed off. Both women knew about the snobbery between people born in Magnolia Hill and those who had moved there. "I know most of them. Nancy Hampton's name ends the list."

"Nancy?" Jillian's heart pounded in her chest. "Stan and I argued about her before his accident. You must have found his client list."

The front door chime interrupted their conversation and made them both jump again. Betty froze, and Jillian put a finger to her lips and shooed her back to the lobby with her hands. She moved behind the desk and stood by the wall. Whoever came in didn't need to know she had entered Stan's office.

Jillian heard Betty say hello, and a male voice answered. She couldn't quite hear, but that didn't last long.

"I told Stan that I wanted my mother's money back. All of it!" Derry Klingman shouted. Betty said something muffled that set him off again.

"What do you mean you don't know where it is? Don't feed me the same line he did. My mother and I called him the day before his accident, and she told him she wanted to make a withdrawal. He said he'd do what he could." Derry caught his breath. "Do what he could?" he snarled. "How dare he say that? My mother can have her money back if she wants it."

Betty murmured again, and Jillian still couldn't hear what she said. Derry didn't sound impressed with her response. "I'll tell you the same thing I told him. You'd better!" Jillian heard the door slam, waited a minute, and then walked into the lobby.

Betty stood behind her desk, sheet white, with eyes full of tears. "Jillian, what am I supposed to do? He wants his mother's money, and I can't help him."

"I don't know what to tell you. I saw him after Stan's funeral, and if looks could kill…" Jillian's voice trailed off.

"Derry's called a couple of times before. He hated it when Stan had gone out or not come in at all, which happened a lot. But he never scared me before. When I'd tell him Stan wasn't there, he'd grumble but leave. Now, he seems dangerous."

"I can understand." Jillian nodded. "I didn't like his threat of 'you'd better.' "

"You don't think he hurt Stan, do you?"

"I have no idea and want to leave that up to the police. I'm more worried about where your boss stashed all his clients' money. So far, we've only found a list of names and a set of notebooks that don't seem useful."

Jillian couldn't imagine how Stan's assistant had been so clueless, but if the frightened woman knew more than she was saying, she didn't show it. She probably couldn't get any more information out of Betty today.

"Do you mind if I take this notebook with me, so I can read it more carefully?" she asked.

"Just be careful. I don't know why the police didn't

take them when they searched Stan's office." At the word police, tears began to stream down Betty's face again, and she wiped them away with the soggy, crumpled tissue she still held.

Jillian gave her a quick hug and started to leave, but then she turned around. "Hey, I don't suppose you know where Stan banked?"

"I do," Betty said simply, and Jillian stared at her in shock. Finally, the clueless admin admitted to knowing something. Betty continued. "He didn't use a national chain. He said he wanted to keep his business local, so he used Sooner Bank. Does that help you?" she asked hopefully.

"More than you can imagine," Jillian assured.

"Will it convince the police that I didn't kill him?"

"Maybe," Jillian said. She didn't want to point out that although Betty's ignorance was frustrating, it provided her with a better defense than knowing too much. "I think the sooner we find the money, the sooner we'll find the murderer."

Jillian stepped out of Stan's office into the bright sun and paused outside to check for messages on her phone. Nothing had come in except for an ad from her feed store. She shook her head, thinking about poor, oblivious Betty.

When she turned toward the lobby one last time, Betty was on the phone. Jillian couldn't hear her words through the glass but saw that she punctuated her thoughts with a forceful arm wave. Jillian hadn't noticed the phone ringing. Had it rung just after she left, or had Betty called someone? A chill ran back down Jillian's spine as she hurried to her truck. Maybe Betty knew more information than she wanted to admit.

Chapter Twenty-Two

The next day, after a quick cup of coffee, Jillian went to Sooner Bank. At least being in finance helped her know most banks' management. She entered the back door of the institution named for people who had broken the rules and entered the state before the Oklahoma land run officially started. Most people heard "Sooners" and thought about football, but Jillian thought the history was more interesting.

Walking down a hallway to the lobby, she saw a full coffeepot that still smelled fresh. She grabbed a small cardboard cup but passed on the donuts, even her favorite cream-filled, not needing to talk to a banker with powdered sugar on her lips. When she entered the main lobby, she checked if Jennifer Browne sat at her desk in one of the side offices. When the vice president saw Jillian, she waved her in.

Jennifer graduated a few years ahead of Jillian and had been a fierce advocate for the planner when she opened her practice. Jennifer's taste in jewelry was legendary. She owned at least a hundred lapel pins that set off her required suits with whimsy and personality. Today, the tall redhead's pin consisted of a mammoth American flag created from rhinestones. It moved the tone of her navy blazer from stuffy to fun in preparation for the 4th.

"Hey, what brings you in this morning?" Jennifer asked.

Jillian cautiously set her coffee beside her, not wanting to spill it on the delicate cherry table, and sat on one of the burgundy leather chairs with low backs that faced Jennifer's desk. She appreciated that it put her at the same height as the banker's chair without sinking three or four inches. She always hated the feeling when she peeked over a desk or table at the person sitting on the other side.

Jillian leaned forward. "I'm glad you're not on vacation because I've got a question I wouldn't want to ask anyone else."

The banker nodded, got up, and closed her office door. Then she sat back down at her desk. "I'll help you if I can."

Jillian knew that although Jennifer had the discretion of a good banker, she also loved a good story. She would know any local financial gossip. "Well, I saw you at Stan's service."

Jennifer shook her head. "Poor guy. I still don't understand his death. How do you lose control of a car on a sunny day?"

"Distracted?" offered Jillian, but when Jennifer shook her head no, she sighed. "I agree it doesn't make sense, and the police don't seem to understand it either. They've decided his death might be suspicious, and they're looking into it further."

"No kidding? Wow! Who would want to kill Stan, other than the women he was stringing along?" Jennifer asked conspiratorially, scanning the bank lobby. Jillian glanced behind her and saw people going about their own days, paying no attention to them. Most people stood in line for tellers and had their backs to Jennifer's office. Additionally, the bank had a loan promotion with red, white, and blue inflated balloons throughout the lobby. The patriotic decoration effectively blocked the view between Jennifer's office and the people standing outside.

"I heard that," Jillian admitted, "but there's something else." She took a sip of her rapidly cooling coffee.

"Really?" Jennifer leaned a little over her desk.

"Yeah, Betty told me that Stan did his banking here."

"I can't confirm that, but I won't deny it either," Jennifer said.

So far, so good, thought Jillian. At least she had come to the right bank. "Great. I know this seems weird, but when I reviewed some documents from Stan's firm, I'm not sure he ran a legitimate financial practice. Honestly, I don't think he invested his clients' money at all."

The smile faded from Jennifer's lips, and she turned white. "What?"

"Well, some of the documents he gave his customers don't make any sense. Then I snooped around his office a little." When Jennifer shot her a questioning glance, Jillian replied, "Don't ask. Anyway, I didn't find any normal paperwork that I would expect him to file. And on top of that, his assistant, Betty, didn't know anything about his practice," she finished. She set down her coffee cup for emphasis.

"You think Stan was running a scam?" Jennifer whispered with a catch in her voice.

"Well, I can't be positive yet, but nothing looks

good. If I'm right, Stan either spent the money or stored it somewhere like a bank. I hope he has a substantial account here." Jillian leaned back a little in her chair.

"Even though I shouldn't, I wish I could help you," Jennifer said. "Stan came into the bank about a year ago and talked to me. He had purchased a piece of software designed to earn good investment returns. He claimed to make at least five percent above the stock market. Stan said that by using the strategy, he couldn't lose money. It sounded appealing." Jennifer's eyes pleaded for Jillian to understand.

The planner's heart sank. Jennifer's name was on the list of clients, too. She never thought to check before she came in. "You gave him money," she said glumly, not even phrasing it as a question.

"I gave him an account I managed, myself. I left most of my money alone, but I gave Stan more than I would want to lose."

Jillian stared down at her chilled cup of coffee. She wanted to scream, but she held her voice level. "Did you notice anything strange about the statements?"

Jennifer's bright red lipstick made a straight line across her face. She looked down, not willing to meet Jillian's gaze. "I didn't pay any attention. The first page showed a monthly profit, and I didn't read any further." Jillian could hear her foot tapping against the plastic chair mat, a sure indicator of the banker's stress. But she needed to learn more and couldn't stop asking questions.

"How did you transfer the money?"

"He had me wire it to him so I would have the receipt. I got my first statement at the end of the month after I opened the account, and I didn't have any reason to doubt him." Jennifer picked up a pen and began to spin it in her right hand, balancing the tip against her left.

"Did he have you fill out any paperwork?"

Jennifer finally made eye contact. "He asked me questions and wrote down my answers. Then he returned a few days later, and I signed the last page of a form."

"Did he give you a copy of it?"

"He asked me if I wanted one," Jennifer said with a shaky tone in her usually confident voice. "I told him I didn't need it."

Jillian knew she had to say something to make her friend feel better. "Don't blame yourself. By asking you if you wanted the paperwork, he gave you confidence that he had set up everything properly."

"He did. I never gave it another thought."

Jillian remembered her clients who had told her they didn't care about paper copies. She insisted on at least emailing PDFs, but she was confident they never opened the messages. Having trusting clients made it easy for Stan to get away with his fraud, especially if he pretended to fill out paperwork. No wonder he had returned to Magnolia Hill, that snake!

"I want you to maintain customer privacy, and you don't have to tell me anything specific, but maybe you can answer this. Given the size of his accounts, would you assume that Stan was wealthy?"

"You're right, Jillian. I can't be specific, but I'd say no. He had money, but not millions of dollars. If he maintained a large account, he didn't keep it here."

Jillian's heart sank. Her search for the money collapsed back to square one.

Chapter Twenty-Three

As Jillian got up to leave Jennifer's office, she leaned across the desk and hugged the shaken banker, promising to share anything she discovered. She walked outside, passing Gayle and Jeff entering the bank. "Hey, officers, anything new?" she asked.

"We're here about Stan's murder. Simply police business, ma'am," Jeff said smugly.

She hated his condescending attitude, and her mouth got the better of her. "You mean you want to see if he stashed the money he stole from the clients in a bank account here?"

The knowing smirk dropped from Jeff's face. "How did you discover that?" he muttered, obviously irritated that Jillian had beaten them to the information. He stared at Gayle. "Did you tell her?"

"Not me! Jilly, how did you know to come to this bank?"

"Just logical civilian thinking, I guess. Good luck." Jillian walked away from them. She knew Gayle would probably chastise her for acting like a smart aleck. If so, she'd manage it. Jeff needed to quit treating her like she was stupid.

Her self-satisfaction withered when she got into her truck and thought more about the exchange with Jeff. If he and Gayle were searching for the money at Sooner

Bank, they didn't know where Stan had deposited it, either. She hoped he hadn't spent it all.

Usually, in Ponzi schemes, the perpetrator had a fantastic, celebrity standard of living. Stan had the swanky yellow Porsche that set him back some, but not at a Maserati-level expense. And although he built his home in the ritziest subdivision, multimillion-dollar mansions didn't exist in Magnolia Hill. Either he had it stashed in another bank account, or he had laundered the money by purchasing something else valuable.

Briefly, she wondered if Stan might have invested his proceeds in cryptocurrency, but she quickly ruled out her idea. Crypto was hard to understand, and although Stan could charm with the best of them, she felt confident he didn't know anything about a blockchain ledger. She assumed he wouldn't even know how to open the account.

On the other hand, the almost invisible funds existed outside most regulations. People operating in the shadows loved the perception of anonymity, even though oversight increased every day. But Jillian could imagine Stan, the center of a crowd at the country club, with a glass of wine in one hand, waving financial dreams with the other. She couldn't imagine him huddled over a computer dressed in a hoodie, ball cap, and sneakers. Most likely, he opened another bank account somewhere else.

Jillian stretched her arms straight out against her steering wheel and sighed. She needed to escape Stan and the lists of people and potential financial ruin. She needed some Agatha time.

She left her briefcase in her car, ran into the house, and changed into her barn jeans that had worn-out cuffs.

She always bought them too long, the right length for riding, so they didn't climb her leg. However, she never remembered to fold them up while walking around, so now, worn half-moons were the result of broken threads. She swapped her blouse for a tank top that said, "Hold Your Horses," and grabbed some socks.

She also found the red, white, and blue streamers for Agatha's mane and tail. Even though the mare had worn them before, Jillian didn't want any surprises, especially after the adventure with Allie.

At the barn, Jillian rejoiced when she pulled her truck into a sliver of shade. Anything that kept the vehicle cooler was welcome, especially when flies forced her to leave the windows up.

Agatha whinnied a happy welcome when she heard Jillian get out of the truck. Maybe it was devotion, or perhaps she just wanted peppermint horse cookies. When Jillian opened the gate, Agatha's nose went into the front pocket of her jeans.

Jillian laughed. "Do you love me or treats?" Agatha squinched her nose and sighed. After she ate the cookies, she licked Jillian's hand for a couple of minutes, an unusual habit that always left her owner sticky. "I'll take that as a both." After Agatha wandered back in front of her fan, Jillian went over to the hose and rinsed off.

She grabbed Agatha's halter, and they walked to the outside arena with the streamers carefully stored in a cloth bag. She kept them wadded up at first and let Agatha sniff them. Then she let her see them unwind. The ever-constant Oklahoma wind soon had the dozen red, white, and blue banners whipping in the breeze. Agatha eyed them carefully, her ears forward, giving them her full attention. Slowly, Jillian brought the streamers toward her. Every time Agatha stepped away, Jillian stopped and let her get used to it. Then she stepped in closer. Eventually, she had the hand holding the streamers on the side of her head. Success!

She wanted to quit on a good note, so she called it an afternoon. Back in her run, Agatha went directly to her feed bowl. Jillian grabbed a scoop of grain and tossed a couple of flakes of Bermuda grass hay into her manger. She topped off her water and kissed her on her nose.

"Do you think I'll ever figure out what happened to the money?"

Agatha nodded yes, either for an answer or because she wanted another cookie.

****

When she got to the front door of her house, Jillian couldn't decide whether to fix something quickly or order a pizza. She reached for the knob, and the door swung open, making her blood run cold. She grabbed her keyring and held it in her fist, keys extending between her second and third fingers. She peered into her house before she quietly stepped through the door. Once inside, she saw drawers, scattered cushions, and paper everywhere. Her trembling fingers almost couldn't dial 911 as she crept farther into her living room to evaluate the damage.

A door slammed hard behind her, and she froze. After what seemed like hours, she turned her head slowly, afraid of what she would see. She started breathing again when she saw no one, only the front door closed. She ran onto her porch, searching up and down the street. Nothing to the left. Nothing to the right.

The 911 operator sounded a million miles away when she asked about the emergency. Jillian sank to the edge of her couch, lifted the phone to her ear, and explained what had happened. The operator asked if she was safe.

"I don't know," she said. "The robber must have still been here but in another room when I arrived. He slammed the door behind me when he left." She listened to the operator ask more questions. "No, there doesn't appear to be anyone else here, and it will take me a long time to figure out what he took. The room's a mess. And I don't see my cat," she cried.

The operator suggested she wait outside, but Jillian ignored her.

"Edgar?" Jillian yelled, looking under the couch. Nothing. "Edgar?" She searched under her table. Still nothing. She ran into her bedroom and found chaos. Dresser drawers lay tossed across the room, and sheets and pillows, torn off the bed, littered the floor. What in the world? "Edgar?" By now, her voice felt tight in her throat, and her words screeched out.

She entered the closet and saw the clothes hanging like she'd left them. She got home before he tossed it. Her legs went limp, and she suddenly felt nauseated, but she had to find the little black cat.

She got down on her knees and flashed her phone's light into the corners. "Edgar?" She heard a tiny rustle and a squeak. In the back of the closet, underneath something that had fallen off a hanger months ago, she saw big yellow eyes.

"Edgar!" Jillian pulled the tiny cat out of the clothes and held him tight while he shook. Then she was afraid.

Chapter Twenty-Four

Jillian stood in her bedroom holding the trembling cat and realized she shouldn't touch anything. She retreated to the living room, carefully stepping over her scattered possessions.

Usually, Edgar would squirm after she picked him up, but today, the black kitty lay still in her arms. She pulled herself together enough to call Allie, who promised to come over with a cat carrier.

Soon, Jillian heard sirens and went outside, still holding Edgar tightly. Gayle and Jeff got out of their cruiser. Gayle rushed up to Jillian and put an arm around her. "We heard the call on the radio, and I wanted to see what happened." She quietly emphasized the word "*I*" and glared at Jeff. "What's going on?"

"I don't know. Somebody broke in and destroyed my place. They tossed my furniture and threw the papers everywhere. I guess the robber hadn't left before I got home because I heard him slam the door after I was already inside." Telling the story again made Jillian queasy, and she leaned a little against the side of her truck.

If Jeff noticed her distress, he didn't comment. "Why do you think the intruder was a man?"

"I don't think anything right now," Jillian snapped. "The footsteps sounded heavy, but it could have been anyone."

"And you didn't see anything?" Gayle asked kindly, ignoring Jeff's eye roll.

"No, I was staring at my living room and heard the door behind me."

"Scary." Gayle glared at Jeff.

"I didn't touch anything other than the front door when I went in. Once I could think, I had to find Edgar, so I moved some clothes in my closet, but that's it." The little cat, feeling braver, offered a soft, appreciative meow.

"Thanks for trying to minimize your impact even though we know your prints will be everywhere," Gayle said. "Do you have any idea why someone would do this?"

Jillian could think of a couple of things and knew she would have to tell them about the thumb drive and the lists. However, Allie's Prius saved her by blowing past two police cars and whipping onto the drive, dangerously close to the trio. Gayle looked amused, but Jeff grumbled and moved away.

Seconds later, Penny's convertible pulled to a less dramatic stop behind the police cars.

They both ran up the drive and grabbed Jillian in a three-way hug while Gayle entered the house with Jeff. Edgar might want to cling to his mom, but this was too much, even for him. He wiggled to get free. Allie backed up, wiping her eyes.

"Oh no, you don't, kitty cat. Your mommy's had enough stress for one day. Hang on. I've got a place for you." She pulled out an enormous cat carrier. Despite the situation, Jillian and Penny laughed.

"Lands sake, Allie, what did you bring? Edgar's not

a lion," Penny said.

"I know. I brought a dog crate. Don't laugh," she said when Penny and Jillian both giggled. "I thought he might like enough room for a blanket and a litter box. I don't know how long until you can return to your house."

"What a good idea," Jillian said. "And I know Edgar will appreciate the space. I wonder if the police would let me get his box?"

Penny hugged Jillian. "You sit down, child. You're still pale as a ghost. I'll ask them. They can't tell an old lady no." She winked.

Penny left to take on the police, and Allie took Edgar out of Jillian's arms and put him in the carrier. The giant door let her set him inside easily. The black cat started sniffing the corners like a new place to explore. After safely depositing Edgar, Allie leaned back against her car.

"Jilly, you need to sit down again. You're green."

"Penny says I'm white, and you say I'm green? I'll be okay," Jillian protested, but she didn't argue.

"Can I drop your tailgate?" Allie continued. "That way, we can sit on it, put Edgar deeper into the bed, and get him out of the sun."

Jillian raised the tonneau cover that protected her truck bed and pulled down the tailgate. She set Edgar inside, where the shadow of the lid kept him shaded.

She hopped up on the back of the truck, and Allie sat beside her.

"Now, tell me what happened," Allie said, rubbing her hair with a blue-painted hand. Just then, Penny emerged with the litter box.

"The police didn't think they would need to hold this for evidence, so now Edgar should be set for a while.

Jillian, do you know what's going on?"

Jillian tried to look at both women at once. "I don't." She told them about running home after lunch, changing clothes, and going to the barn.

"Did the thief take anything?" Allie asked.

"I don't think so. Maybe he wanted something specific." The three women each expressed alarm in her way. Penny's eyebrows drew together, Allie's eyes opened wide, and Jillian's left leg swung back and forth while she sat.

She continued. "They didn't want jewelry because they didn't open the chest, but they emptied all the drawers in my bedroom and living room. They even threw my pillows and bedding on the floor."

"Do you keep any cash in your house?" Penny asked.

"Maybe twenty bucks, but nothing worth the robbery. Of course, they might not have known it before they broke in."

"Guns?"

"I keep an antique rifle in my garage that could be considered a collector's item. I don't know if they took it. And everyone knows I hate painkillers, so if they're local, they shouldn't have been searching for drugs. I only have a five-year-old bottle of something they gave me when I broke my arm."

Penny glanced over at the police officers walking in and out of Jillian's home and turned her back to them. "Where's the thumb drive?" she asked quietly.

"In the center console of my truck, at the bottom. I figured no one would think to check there. Looks like I made a good decision."

"But, Jilly, how would anyone know you had it?"

"Well, I've talked about Stan to Kandace, Grady, Betty, Derry, Marge, Jennifer, and Gayle. Who knows how many people they told? Maybe whoever broke into my house wanted the thumb drive, or maybe they think I have some other information about Stan."

"You told Gayle, and she let you keep it?" Allie asked.

"Not about the thumb drive, just the weird investment statements. It shook her because even her grandmother worked with Stan."

"That takes nerve," Penny tsked. "To steal from the grandmother of a police officer. Why would someone care that you're trying to get to the bottom of it?" She wiped the sweat off her forehead. The Oklahoma heat was relentless even though the sun was near the horizon.

Jillian tended to forget Penny's age. She acted forty but was more than thirty years older than that. She patted the tailgate beside her. "Come sit down by me. I hate that you're caught up in this, too."

Penny shook her head. "No need. I'm more confused about this robbery than anything else."

"Maybe Stan had an accomplice," Jillian wondered. "Maybe someone else helped him, and they think I've found something implicating them."

"You think Stan had a partner?" Allie asked.

"It makes sense," Jillian said. "Stan didn't strike me as the sharpest tool in the shed." Loud voices coming from the house made them all turn.

Gayle and Jeff came down the drive. "We've called forensics, and they're going to dust for prints. Did anyone know you would be gone this afternoon?" Gayle asked.

"Most of my friends know I go to the barn nearly

every afternoon. If I'm home, I park the truck on the drive. Anyone could figure out my schedule."

Jeff glared at her. "Why would anyone care about your schedule or break into your house? Are you sticking your nose in police business again?"

Gayle sighed. "C'mon, Jeff. Dial it back a little."

"I will not," Jeff huffed. "You know civilians have no business in police investigations. I hear you've been asking questions about Stan's death. Gayle said you told her that Stan might have lied to his clients, and her information caused the department to take another look at his accident. I disagreed, but no one listened to me." He glared again at Gayle and pushed his hat back on his head, showing a sweating brow and receding hairline. "Stan just got distracted and went off the road. Nothing but a plain and simple tragedy."

"I know you liked Stan," Gayle said, "but if he cheated his clients, his death seems a little convenient."

"Stan was a genius," Jeff said. "I needed some of my money back, and he gave it to me. I never saw any bad behavior, and I never had any problems." He punched the word "I" each time, like that explained everything. "And I always earned solid returns. I don't know how I'll replace him. You sure you just ain't jealous?"

"No, Officer Stone." Jillian adopted an overly formal tone and sighed. "And I'm not interfering in your investigation. I just think Stan's business actions don't make sense. They're set up like a Ponzi scheme, even if you're the lucky one getting money back."

"How do you figure?" Jeff asked despite himself.

"The con provides requested funds for as long as he can. It keeps people from getting suspicious. Eventually, the distributions become more difficult or impossible, especially if the scammer spends the money, or a market event spooks people."

"Whatever," Jeff muttered. "You sure nothing's missing?"

"Of course not," Jillian said tersely. "I haven't touched anything. I couldn't until you got here."

"Well, check it out after we leave, and tell us if anything's gone. Come on, Gayle. We gotta get back to the station when forensics shows up." He stomped off, and Gayle gave an apologetic smile.

"Jillian, can you go to Allie's for a while? I'll call you when we're finished."

"No problem," Jillian answered. She needed to tell Gayle about the thumb drive but wouldn't say anything in front of Jeff. What a jerk!

Chapter Twenty-Five

After much protesting by her friends, Jillian convinced them that she could take her truck to Allie's house. However, her hands began shaking once she set Edgar's carrier in the back seat and put the truck in reverse. She finally got the gear in drive and made her way down the street. Even though she knew the danger was over, she was still terrified. The white-hot day had finally given way to purple dusk, and she struggled to drive and watch behind her. Finally, she pulled up to Allie's gated condo community. She punched in the code and watched the reassuring gate close behind her without a tail.

Allie's unit stood out from the other dark gray condos. Brightly colored metal animals with springs for necks and tails peeked around the riotous flowers in her garden, and the corner of her front porch held a Talavera vase purchased on a recent vacation to Mexico. The vivid pottery filled with marigolds coordinated with ceramic lizards climbing up her wall.

Allie had beaten her again. She emerged from her Prius and helped Jillian carry her briefcase, Edgar, and the thumb drive. The black cat usually didn't mind the truck, but tonight, he had sung ungodly yowls for most of the drive, adding to Jillian's stress. She thought he should stay in Allie's rental palace for the evening. He seemed too upset to explore a new area. Allie's calico cat, Chloe, approached the carrier, peered in, and sniffed. Then she wandered off with no warning hiss. Her mild temper surprised Jillian because Chloe didn't suffer fools lightly, but Edgar's mom also knew animals could read each other. Chloe seemed to realize that, at least tonight, Edgar was no threat. For his part, the black cat sat on his haunches in the middle of the carrier where Chloe's inquisitive paw couldn't reach him. Eventually, he lay in a tight circle, one eye above his tail, to watch Chloe and his mom.

Allie opened a Mexican beer for Jillian, poured it into a tall glass, and added a wedge of lime. Jillian took a deeper drink than usual and set the glass down, three-quarters full, and sighed.

"Feeling a little better, sweet girl?" Penny asked kindly.

"I can't seem to stop shaking." She held out her hand, and even though the trembling had lessened, she still had an obvious tremor. "Someone broke into my house, tore up my stuff, and somehow, Officer Stone seems mad at me about it."

"Jeff seemed overly defensive, didn't he?" the older woman mused.

"For sure," Allie agreed. "I wonder why he supported Stan so much."

"I don't know," answered Jillian. "But did you notice how he kept asking if I was missing anything? How could I answer that if I called the police immediately?"

"Some men just can't be wrong," Penny said, "and if Jeff worked with Stan, he might bristle at a group of women calling him a victim."

"I've known guys like that," Allie murmured, then her eyes widened. "You don't think Jeff was 'working working' with Stan, was he?" She put air quotes around the repeated words.

Jillian leaned forward. "You mean helping him with the con? What a strange twist, especially since all the police except Jeff seem intent on fingering Betty for the killer. You'd think he would embrace that theory or any other that cleared his name. I don't know. The idea that Jeff killed Stan seems pretty farfetched. I think Betty seems like the most logical person to be Stan's accomplice."

"Maybe the police think Betty killed Stan because she did," Penny offered. "Usually, the most logical answer is accurate."

"Maybe," Jillian admitted. "Of course, she also could have helped him with the con but not been the killer. Someone else, like an angry client, might have gotten revenge."

"At least the robber ran off when he heard you." Penny shuddered. "A little different string of events, and tonight could have ended badly."

A cold chill ran through Jillian again. "I know I have to give Gayle the thumb drive. I can't keep avoiding it, especially now, but tonight I just couldn't with Jeff's attitude."

"Don't let your pride get you hurt," Penny cautioned.

All three of them jumped when the doorbell rang. "Oh, I forgot to tell you that I ordered pizza," Allie said, extricating herself from Chloe and a pile of bright-colored throw pillows on her striped couch. Soon, she returned to the family room with two large pies—a pepperoni and a combination.

The pizza provided a delicious diversion from their serious conversation. The crust showed slightly charred marks from the wood stove, and the tangy tomato sauce didn't overpower the meat or fresh onions, bell peppers, and mushrooms.

Jillian reached for a second slice and enviously remembered girls who said, "Oh, I'm so stressed. I can't eat a thing." She had never said that. She stayed slim because she did too much barn work. Still, no one who knew her ever said she had the appetite of a bird unless that bird was a vulture!

Allie turned to Jillian. "If you're right about the thumb drive, the killer will know he didn't find what he wanted. What makes you think he won't come back?"

"I could hope he decides I don't have anything he wants, but that seems risky. I'll make it harder for him by purchasing an alarm system tomorrow." Jillian took another sip of beer. "But tonight, I also need to check my office. Maybe whoever broke into my house will want to search it, too, to see if I left the drive there. A robbery could cause my clients' identities to get hacked, and the damage control would take months."

"I'll go with you," Allie said, her second beer making her brave.

Jillian started to protest, but Penny interrupted. "I think Allie should go, but you should drive. You've only had one beer, right?"

"Not even." Jillian held up her glass, still half full. "I knew I'd have to get home."

Allie got up and grabbed her purse. "Let's go now. It will only get scarier the later it gets. You don't mind watching Edgar for a while?" she asked her grandmother.

"Not at all," Penny assured. "Edgar and I are good friends."

Edgar huddled his body like he didn't have any friends. He had not moved from the middle of his cage, and he jumped at any sound. They had offered him cat food, cat treats, and even pepperoni from the pizza. Nothing enticed him. Jillian reached into the middle of the cage and rubbed under his neck, and he stretched out a little. "Don't be afraid, Edgar. I'll come back in a few minutes."

When they headed out the door, Penny called a warning. "You girls stay safe. If anything, and I mean anything, seems off, call the police. Do not go in there by yourself. You hear me?"

They turned around, and each kissed the woman on the cheek. "Loud and clear," Jillian said. "I've had enough stress for one evening."

As they drove downtown, Jillian asked, "Hey, can you check in my glove box for my gun?"

Allie reached around in the dark, and her eyes got big when she pulled out the .45. "Jillian, I thought you said you didn't own a handgun."

"No, I said I didn't have a gun at the house. I've had this for several years. I don't like carrying it, but I like surprises in the dark even less. I moved it back into my truck after Stan died." She turned onto the street in front of her office.

Usually, Jillian found the location beautiful, whether during the business day or evening. Tonight, though, it seemed spooky and deserted. The downtown streetlamps created both shadows and light. The leaves on the trees danced like dark, moving shapes on the sides of the buildings, producing a sense of movement everywhere, even with no one around.

Approaching the door, Jillian saw a dark shape moving through the shadows, approaching them quickly. She threw a protective arm in front of Allie and pulled the gun out of her pocket.

Chapter Twenty-Six

The movement of the person and the shadows made her dizzy. Which shapes were real, and which were just imagined? Slowly, a figure began to emerge, but the bad light hid his features. Jillian's fingers tightened around the gun handle as the person moved closer. What would she do? She had shot plenty of targets, but could she shoot someone? She always thought she could, but suddenly, she didn't know. She wished she had her cell phone instead. She knew she could dial 911.

"Jillian? Allie? What are y'all doing downtown?" Will Anderson stepped out from the shadows. He stared down at Jillian's hand and quickly raised frightened eyes back at her. "Woah, woah, woah. Don't shoot! Put the gun down. It's me, Will."

Jillian was beyond relieved to recognize the dark figure, even if it was Will. She exhaled, unaware until then that she had been holding her breath, took her finger off the trigger, and lowered the gun to her side. "Will, you scared me to death! What are you doing here?"

"I work here, remember?" Will said, pointing to the newspaper office around the corner. "I had to work late to meet a deadline and walked here to find something to eat. I was about to go into the bar two up from you. But why are you here, and why do you have a gun? You both look like you've seen a ghost."

"Someone broke into Jillian's home and tossed it. We needed to check on her office," Allie said, ignoring her friend's glare.

"At least that explains the gun." He nodded at the .45, running his hand through his dark, curly hair.

"I needed to protect myself in case something went wrong," she said.

Will's green eyes narrowed. "Why did someone break into your house, and why do you think they might be at your office?"

Allie started to speak, but Jillian shook her head. "I don't need to read about it in the paper. Everything's fine."

"Like a Louise Penny 'fine'?" Will asked, and Jillian smiled. Penny, one of Jillian's favorite authors, used the word "fine" to suggest anything but.

"Maybe not that fine, but I've got it," she said, moving through the shadows past Will. Allie shrugged at Will and followed Jillian.

"Jilly, wait," Will called out. Jillian stopped. "At least let me walk through your office with you. Even if you won't tell me anything, I can't leave you here ready to kill someone you find inside."

"Oh, I don't intend to kill him," Jillian said. "I just want to scare him real bad."

"Even so, please let me come with you?" Usually arrogant Will appeared so concerned that Jillian nodded her head. She didn't want to thank him, but she appreciated having someone else along, especially someone tall who looked like he worked out.

When they got to the main door, Jillian was relieved to see it still closed and undisturbed. She used the flashlight on her phone to find the keyhole and quickly let them inside.

She knew she needed to bring the gun into the office, but the presence in her hand didn't make her feel more comfortable. Only after they stood inside with the lobby lights on and the doors locked did she feel safer, and she immediately laid the gun down. Then all three went into each room and turned on the lights to keep the shadows at bay as they progressed from the offices to the storage room, conference room, kitchen, and bathrooms.

They carefully crept through the offices like they were in a murder mystery movie, and Jillian knew their progress showed through the large windows. She wished that one of them had an oversized magnifying glass. She hoped that if anyone considered breaking in, all the activity might make them think twice.

A robbery was one of Jillian's biggest nightmares, behind fire and a tornado. Even though the office had a sturdy external deadbolt and a separate lock on the file room door, she had enough information on her clients that criminals could easily steal identities if they obtained access. Fortunately, everything appeared untouched.

When they finished, Will leaned long legs against Katherine's desk in the lobby and stared at Jillian, the gold flecks in his green eyes flashing. "Now, will you tell me what's going on?" He rubbed his hand against his chin, and she heard the scraping. Even though he tried to be clean-shaven, the dark stubble was obvious. She hadn't paid any attention to him for years. Had he always been handsome?

Jillian couldn't meet his gaze. She didn't want to tell Will anything, even though he probably deserved a little explanation after he postponed dinner for her. But any information she gave him needed to come with conditions.

"Fair enough. First, I know you are always on the hunt for your next story. Why should I trust that you won't publish it tomorrow if I tell you something tonight?"

Will didn't answer immediately, considering her question. Then his eyes twinkled. "Because tomorrow's paper has already gone to press?"

"Very funny," she said. "I've just got to know that I can trust you. You don't have a great history with that." Will's eyes dropped, and he reddened slightly, but Jillian continued. "If I tell you any of this, do you promise— Scout's honor—that you won't go to press on it?"

Will crossed his heart. "Scout's honor. Of course, you know I was never a scout."

"Typical." Jillian tightened her lips.

The light died in Will's eyes. "Hey, hey, okay. I promise on any honor you want. I won't publish anything we talk about tonight."

She looked back at him. "I appreciate your help and feel I owe you an explanation."

"Even if you didn't tell me anything, I couldn't leave you to die at the hands of an intruder. I'm a nicer person than that," laughed Will. "Maybe not much nicer, but still... Hey, eventually, could I have an exclusive if it turns into something?" he asked after a pause.

"That seems fair," Jillian said, still dubious.

"Would y'all mind talking back at my house?" Allie asked. "I hate to leave *Babcia* there by herself for a long time. I think everyone's nerves are a little frayed tonight."

"No problem," Will said and gave Jillian his phone

number. "Send me her address, and I'll meet you there."

"Hey, why didn't you give me your cell?" Allie asked.

Will grinned at Allie and spoke again to Jillian. "Send me her address, and I'll meet you there."

Chapter Twenty-Seven

Jillian and Allie headed home, riding silently with the .45 safely back in the glove box.

Finally, Allie spoke. "Sheesh, I'm glad you didn't shoot Will. I didn't recognize him at first, and I hate to admit that I felt better knowing you had your gun."

Jillian laughed. "I'm glad you felt safe, but I didn't. Don't look surprised," she said at Allie's raised eyebrows. "When it mattered, I realized I couldn't shoot someone. I wished I'd had my phone in my hand instead. Maybe I should trade my gun for some mace. I'm sure I could shoot that."

"Hmm," Allie said thoughtfully. "You always act so confident that I never considered you would hesitate to shoot if you had to do it. Mace might be a good purchase for both of us. Maybe Will could buy some for you." Allie glanced sideways at her friend.

Jillian shot her a dirty look. "I don't want Will buying me anything. I'll get it for myself," she said as she pulled into Allie's driveway. "And I'll pick up some for you, too."

Will drove up in his multicolored, classic Mustang. Jillian studied the patchwork paint job and assumed he was in the process of restoring the car. If not, he had a strange sense of style.

When Jillian and Allie got out of the truck, Penny

opened the door and unconsciously put her hand to her throat. "Lands sake, girls, I'm glad to see you. You were gone a little longer than I expected." She stopped as Will walked up the drive. "Will Anderson, good to see you again. How's your mom and grandmother?"

"They're both fine, Miss Penny," Will said. "I'll tell them you asked after them. How about you?"

"Busy," she answered. She searched Allie's face for an explanation.

"Will was walking downtown in front of Jillian's office, and she almost shot him," Allie started. Penny's face contorted, and she tried to contain a laugh.

"I did not," Jillian insisted. "I wanted my gun when I went into my office, and Will startled us. I didn't come anywhere near shooting him."

"Well, good deal," Penny summed up.

"I didn't want them checking out Jilly's office alone after they told me about the robbery," Will said. "Not that they needed any help," he quickly added when he saw Jillian's expression.

"Anyway, they promised to tell me what was going on, but we wanted to come back here so you wouldn't worry." He held the door for everyone to walk into Allie's condo.

Penny nodded. "I surely appreciate that. Come on in, then. There's still a little pizza left that we can rewarm."

"Sounds good," he said. "I was headed to dinner when I saw them."

Jillian couldn't decide how much to tell Will, and she figured either she trusted him, or she didn't. If she didn't trust him, she shouldn't tell him anything. But he had seemed genuinely worried about them. Maybe he'd grown up a little.

She bent down to pet Edgar. "How's kitty?" she asked Penny.

"He'll be all right once he gets home," the older woman answered. "I don't think he moved a muscle after you left. Chloe's sniffed the cage a couple of times, but she's ignoring him." When Chloe heard her name, she jumped off the couch and trotted over to Penny, who rubbed her behind her ears.

While Will polished off the last of the combination pizza, Jillian explained Stan's unorthodox investment statements and the documents she had found in his desk drawer. At the last minute, she omitted the thumb drive. Penny and Allie obviously noticed but didn't say anything.

"Wow, you've turned into quite the crime fighter," he said, wiping tomato sauce off his mouth. "How much have you told the police?"

"I told Gayle about the investment statements and that I thought someone killed Stan."

"What did she say?"

"Not a lot at the time, but she believed me. She told me even her grandmother was one of Stan's clients." Jillian shook her head sadly. "After she and I talked, the police reopened an investigation into his death. Of course, Jeff's mad. He thinks their efforts are a waste of time."

"Jeff's a pain in the neck." Will laughed. "He tells me all the time that I have no business asking him questions, and I keep reminding him of freedom of the press. I know *The Magnolia Daily*'s small potatoes, but he doesn't need such a belligerent attitude."

"I agree," Jillian said, ignoring Penny and Allie

exchanging amused glances at the friendly conversation she was having with Will. Jillian shot a fast glare at them and continued. "I think Stan's fraud is related to his accident."

Will nodded in agreement. "I went to the crash scene when I heard it on the police radio. It was still early evening when I got there, so his vision couldn't have been an issue. No rain. No brake or skid marks. Randomly, he just lost control."

Everyone knew Will loved to work on cars, and Jillian decided to take advantage of his knowledge. "Could someone have tampered with the car?"

"The police ruled out the obvious ways. No one cut the brake lines or made some obvious mechanical alterations. Of course, the insurance agents haven't finished their review yet, but I trust Grady."

"I do, too, but could there be another way? I don't know, like some James Bond method of disabling a car?" Jillian smiled when she said it, but Allie and Penny knew she wasn't kidding.

Will opened his mouth, shook his head, and closed it again. "No, that's not reasonable." He seemed to answer himself.

"What?" Jillian asked.

"Well, if we've moved to the level of a James Bond-style murder, it might be possible for someone to take control of the car remotely."

"You mean, with some sort of device?" Allie asked.

"Sort of," Will said, "but these bad guys can gain control just by using implanted software."

"Merciful heavens! I've never heard of anything like that," Penny said, leaning forward on the red chair where she sat.

Jillian paused for a moment. "I have, but more from a theoretical perspective while I was researching a software company. The automotive industry has major concerns about it."

"One of the biggest cybersecurity initiatives right now," Will agreed.

"But wouldn't it be difficult to pull off?" Allie asked while she got packaged pecan sandies out of her pantry.

"Not like you'd think," he answered. "It's frighteningly simple. If someone wanted to, they could download a virus onto whatever the owner used to update the vehicle."

"Update the vehicle?" Penny asked, reaching for a cookie. "I don't have updates, and I drive a nice car."

"You drive a very nice convertible," Will agreed. "But it's a few years old. High-end, new cars…"

"Like Stan's Porsche…" Jillian interrupted.

"Like Stan's Porsche," Will repeated, "download updates, primarily for their entertainment and navigation system. However, you could also upload a virus onto the same device."

"You mean a device like a thumb drive?" Jillian asked quietly.

Allie swore and then studied her grandmother's face nervously. Penny's eyes crinkled, and she patted her granddaughter's hand.

"Maybe a thumb drive. Why?" Will asked.

Jillian went to her briefcase. She pulled out the monogrammed thumb drive. "You mean something like this?"

"Where did you get that?" Will asked.

"Can we leave it at I found it?" Jillian asked. No way would she tell Will how she'd acquired the thumb drive.

"Are you sure it's Stan's?"

"Yes. Check out the initials. Also, I know his files are on it."

"I can assume you opened the drive." Will sounded incredulous.

"You're close, but let's get back to what you just said. He has a folder on this drive that has files for his car. Do you know what his update files would look like?"

"I might. Can I see it?"

Since Allie had already checked the drive for viruses, Jillian got her computer from her briefcase and set it on Allie's white tile kitchen counter. She opened the lid, inserted the thumb drive, and turned the computer on. Will stood over her shoulder while Allie and Penny stood to the side. She quickly opened the Porsche folder before Will could see any other documents. Then she slid the laptop to her left, so he could sit directly in front of it. Then she watched him skim the files. He ran his left hand through his hair while he scrolled through lines of code with his right, until he stopped and let out a low whistle.

"Okay, this is weird."

"What?" Jillian, Allie, and Penny asked at the same time.

"Lines of code were altered," Will said.

"What does that even mean?" Penny asked.

"Well, I'm not sure. Maybe nothing. But it looks like someone added lines of code that included an auto-delete function. They left a gap."

"You mean lines of code like a virus?" Jillian asked.

"Well, I can't be sure, but I know that auto-deletion isn't common in these files. Maybe someone better at forensics would know how to retrieve the information."

"I guess I better talk to Gayle Johnson." Jillian sighed. "Jeff will hit the roof."

"You didn't steal it from the police station, did you?" Will asked. He laughed and then sounded concerned. "Did you?"

"Of course not," Jillian said.

"Then they missed it, and they should be grateful that you paid more attention than they did."

Jillian was glad Will saw it that way, and she felt considerably better. Maybe he wasn't a complete jerk after all. And standing that close to him, she couldn't help but notice that he smelled good—soap and the hint of a woodsy fragrance she didn't recognize. Guys who smelled like the cologne counter of a department store didn't do it for her.

She pushed opinions about Will's cologne aside. Even though he appeared to have grown up, she didn't believe people changed personalities, even if they matured. Will was useful for information, but that was all.

Penny moved closer to the laptop. "If you're right, Will, doesn't that limit the number of people who could have put the virus on the drive? They'd need access to his keys, right? I'm assuming he kept the thumb drive on his key ring."

"Probably," Jillian said, "but I know at the time of the accident, the thumb drive and the keys weren't attached."

"He'd probably just updated his car and hadn't put the drive back on the chain yet. And you'd think the drive would limit the number of people," Will agreed, "but there's a problem."

Penny raised her eyebrows at him. Allie had come

by that quirk naturally, Jillian thought. Will continued. "Stan auctioned off his car two weeks ago for an Alzheimer's fundraiser because his grandmother died from an early onset version of the disease when she was sixty-five. Even though he didn't live here then, we ran the obituary. You know how small-town papers work."

"I don't remember seeing it," Penny said.

"Well, the write-up wasn't very long since she didn't live here. I know many people read the obits daily, but you could have missed hers."

Penny laughed. "I hate to sound morbid, but when you get to be my age, you don't want to miss somebody."

"Ewww, *Babcia*," Allie screeched.

Will continued. "His car and keys sat on display at the farmer's market for three or four hours last week. The thumb drive was on the key ring, along with a giant tag saying 'Stop Alzheimer's.' I saw them hanging up on a hook like part of the marketing. He put the event out all over social media. People should come by, donate, and receive a raffle ticket for the chance to use his car for an evening. Someone could have brought a laptop and downloaded the virus quickly onto the drive."

"But wouldn't he miss the keys?" Jillian asked. Will was standing very close to her as they both read the laptop screen, and she could feel the heat from his arm radiating against hers. The sensation wasn't unpleasant.

Either Will didn't notice her paying attention to him, or he thought she was focusing on his words when he paused for a minute. And just like that, Stan's death took over her mind again. "If I were going to do it," offered Will, "I'd have brought a different key fob and hung it up. I bet no one would notice."

"I saw his display, too," Penny said. "I love to go to

the farmer's market, especially this time of year. I know older southern women grow tomatoes, at least according to the movies, but I'd rather buy them every Saturday. I'm no farmer, but I'm a great farmer's marketer. And I love having lunch at one of the new food trucks."

"Did you see Stan?" Jillian asked.

Penny nodded her head slowly. "When I walked by, no one stood at the booth. But Stan and Gina were close, eating burgers at a picnic table beside a food truck just past his car."

"Gina was with him?"

"I didn't know who she was then, but I noticed her style seemed very high-end for a Saturday morning. Her clothing and shoes are memorable."

"No kidding," Jillian agreed. "I'm surprised he left the keys to his Porsche unsupervised."

"Stan and Gina would have been close enough to watch everything," Penny explained. "He parked the car beside the tent, and no one could steal it without running over people. I'm sure they weren't worried about someone just taking the keys."

"Anyone who attended the market could have planted a virus on the thumb drive." Jillian sighed.

"Looks that way," Will agreed.

"Why didn't the car crash that day? He drove it longer," Allie said, reaching for another cookie. Chloe also liked cookies and jumped on her owner's lap, trying to pry it out of her hand with a determined, dainty paw. The artist lifted the treat high over her head, and eventually, Chloe jumped down. The whole time, Edgar just stared.

"Of course, we don't know someone tampered with the car at the farmer's market," reminded Will.

"However, the virus could have had a date trigger and GPS coordinates."

"That would guarantee when and where he would lose control, so his car would go over the cliff," Jillian said.

"And explain the lack of brake or skid marks. He couldn't control the Porsche," Will finished.

Jillian shuddered. "That seems like a gruesome way to kill someone. Stan must have been terrified." Penny and Allie nodded.

"It certainly seems like someone wanted him dead," Will said. "They went to a lot of trouble and took some risks."

"Are there video cameras near the farmer's market?" Penny asked.

"I don't know," Jillian said. "I'll check tomorrow. I don't suppose either of you noticed anyone at the market."

"Everyone goes," Penny said. "I saw Derry. He always gives away seven-day coupons for dry cleaning. If I stop by his booth every weekend, I always keep a new discount."

"Derry Klingman? Okay, anybody else?"

"Betty had a big bag of produce. I commented on her fresh lettuce, and she showed me the booth where she bought it. I also saw several friends, but I can't imagine them rigging a thumb drive."

"No, I can't see that either, Penny, although your friends are sharp. Don't eliminate them too soon!" Jillian laughed.

"You're too kind. Oh, and Gayle and Jeff were supposedly security, but I swear Jeff only goes for the free food the vendors give him." Penny laughed, but then her eyes grew serious. "I declare, you shouldn't need security at a farmer's market."

Just then, Jillian's cell phone buzzed, and everyone jumped. She checked her notifications.

"Speaking of Gayle, she just messaged me that the police have finished examining my house, and I can come home."

She typed a reply, and soon, the phone buzzed again. "She said she'll wait until I come back so that she can give me my keys. I think I better head that way."

"Do you want someone to go with you?" Allie asked.

"No, if Gayle's still there, I'll know nobody else got in the house."

"Do you have a deadbolt and a chain?" Will asked.

"I do, for both the front and back doors. I suspect they're intact because I only used the thumb bolt when I left. And I can kill the power to my garage door from inside. Don't worry," she said with more confidence than she felt to the three concerned faces.

"Let me know when you're home safe," Allie said.

"Me, too," Penny agreed.

"Me, three," Will echoed.

"I will. I'll text all of you."

"Thanks," Will said. "Save my number."

Chapter Twenty-Eight

With a big, inauthentic grin to her friends, Jillian picked up Edgar's carrier and her briefcase and drove home. Will had offered again to follow her, but she didn't want to impose on him any more than she already had. He had stepped up to the plate tonight, and he smelled good, but her old dislike of him still burned hot. Even so, she saved his number.

She also kept glancing behind her. Had the same set of headlights followed her since she left Allie's? No, it turned into the grocery store. What about the car behind it? Every PI show she had seen involved tailing a car by staying two to three vehicles behind. No, the second car pulled off at the Stop 'n' Go. She felt sweat running down the back of her shirt.

Finally, she made it back home and squeezed the pickup into the garage. Usually, she preferred to park on her drive because her Ford was so long, but tonight, she sucked in her breath and continued to pull forward until her front grill almost touched the deep freeze. She even hit the key fob after she got out. No one was tampering with her truck!

When she stepped outside, she was relieved to see her uniformed friend waiting on her drive. Gayle gave her a quick hug, along with a pet for Edgar, through the bars of the carrier.

"Here's your keys. I promise no one is inside. We even went through your attic."

"And the Christmas ornaments I need to toss out?"

"The police force isn't judgy." Gayle laughed. "But if you ever wanted a garage sale, you could help two or three families celebrate the holidays with your leftovers."

"I'll keep that in mind," Jillian said, almost forgetting for a minute why they were standing on her driveway after midnight. She suspected Gayle had made the crack for that reason.

"Is Jeff here with you?" Jillian asked.

"No, he caught a ride back with the forensics team. He didn't want to hang around and wait for you. I know you're disappointed." Gayle laughed again and headed toward her squad car.

Fear and guilt stopped Jillian from making much of a wisecrack. Instead, she took a deep breath and called the officer back.

"Hey, if you've got a minute, I need to talk to you."

Gayle stopped walking to her squad car and turned around. "Sure. What's up?"

"I found something I should have told you about a few days ago." Jillian dropped her eyes, kicking the ground a little with her boot. "I tried a couple of times, but Jeff always riled me up."

Gayle sighed. "This doesn't sound good. What did you find?"

"Stan's thumb drive."

Gayle's shock showed in the screech of her voice. "What? Where?"

"His car."

"How did you get access to the Porsche?"

"I saw it at Grady's. Don't blame him—he didn't know I took anything. I went by the morning after the accident, and y'all had already removed his items. Grady said the insurance company was coming to tow the car away. I noticed something shiny and saw the thumb drive wedged deep in the front seat."

"You know not to touch evidence, and you also know you should have given us the drive immediately. I swear, Jillian, sometimes…"

"It wasn't evidence because, at Kandace's, you told me his death was only an accident after you'd already searched the car. The drive would have gotten lost if I hadn't found it."

"Jeff's gonna love this," Gayle grumbled.

"Yes, I know, but wait 'til you hear what I found."

"Let me guess. Information that showed his fraud, right?"

"Some of it, but we found more than that. Will was talking…"

Gayle interrupted her. "Will? Now you've got the newspaper involved?"

"I didn't mean for that to happen. It's a long story, and I thought he was a mugger, so I almost shot him, and then he helped me search my office, so I had to tell him what happened, and anyway, he's promised not to run anything until you give the okay." Jillian caught her breath after her rundown of the evening's events.

Gayle glared at her, and Jillian offered a contrite smile. That last part of her explanation hadn't exactly happened, but Will had promised to wait. Jillian didn't think he would betray a trust like that.

Gayle obviously disagreed and snorted at Will's promise. "Just tell me what he found."

"Will thinks someone put a virus on Stan's hard drive that disabled the car when it reached a certain map position."

Gayle stared at her like she was crazy. "Seriously? I've seen better plots in B-rated spy movies."

"Don't dismiss him so quickly. He reviewed the files for the car, and someone deleted a section of the code. Why would they do that?"

"I don't know," Gayle admitted.

"And it would explain why Stan drove off the road without being on his phone or struggling with driving conditions."

"Do you have the thumb drive?"

Jillian pulled the plastic bag containing the monogrammed block out of her pocket. "Here it is. No one has touched it without using a tissue. I'm sorry," she said to the grim officer. "I just wanted to find files to prove whether or not Stan had cheated his clients."

"And you found something?"

"I did. I was going to contact the Department of Securities today, but I got busy. I've also been trying to find the money if he didn't spend it all."

"Jillian, stop interfering," Gayle scolded, motioning at the planner's front door. "Look at your house. Someone knows you're snooping around, and they want you to stop. The police will find Stan's killer, especially if they have access to *all* the data, including information from the thumb drive you couldn't find because they are trained professionals." Gayle's voice grew louder with each word, and Jillian couldn't miss the sarcasm in her voice.

"I was always going to give it to you," she protested. "I hope you can catch whoever broke into my house."

Her voice wasn't confident, and her anxiety unnerved her more than the break-in.

"We're checking nearby home video systems. You didn't have one?"

Jillian shook her head.

Gayle sighed at her friend sympathetically. "I appreciate your dedication. I know you do all this for your grandmother, and I'm grateful you're now fighting for mine. I'll keep you in the loop quietly, but back off. For your own safety, stay out of this."

"I will. I can get a little extra when I get wound up." She hugged Gayle, watched her pull out of her driveway, and stepped into her house before the officer drove out of sight.

Jillian immediately locked the thumb bolt and the deadbolt and fastened the chain. Then she pulled all the drapes. She usually didn't do that in the living room, but she didn't want someone watching her tonight.

Finally, she let Edgar out of Allie's palace and put his litter box back in her bathroom, where she kept it. He followed her and immediately used it. Cats. Oh well, they had tried to keep him comfortable. She poured some dry food into his bowl and headed into the living room to tackle the disaster.

Besides picking up papers and a few mystery paperbacks, she mostly replaced drawers and uprighted her kitchen chairs. The robbery appeared to be a search for something she would have hidden. Whoever broke in had to be looking for the thumb drive.

In the excitement of everything, she realized she had forgotten to tell anyone about the notebook she had taken from Stan's office. It would have to wait until she had righted her world.

She knew she couldn't fall asleep, so she worked until she had everything returned to its correct spot. Then she carefully wiped off the fingerprint powder with a dry paper towel, a small brush, and a dustpan. She was relieved that the officers had carefully avoided her brown leather furniture, but the cleanup took forever.

Once she put the living room together, she went back to the garage. She had parked quickly, not checking for damage, in her hurry to talk with Gayle. Sure enough, her antique rifle hung on the wall, expensive tools still lay on the workbench, and her bicycle and golf clubs sat untouched. The person who broke in wasn't a common burglar.

Jillian sighed, knowing she couldn't go to bed soon. She went into the kitchen to make a pot of coffee. The kitchen drawers appeared unscathed, and the appliances held their normal places on her counter, but she still washed the coffeepot with soap. The idea that someone had searched her house—*her. house.*—left her shaken.

She washed her favorite coffee cup featuring a headshot of Agatha in turquoise tack. She suspected she would scrub everything for a while. On her best day, she was a bit of a germaphobe.

Even though she had closed the blinds, locked the doors, and the temperature still hovered in the 80s, she felt cold and shaky inside. She hadn't turned on the television and heard all the night's noises. Popping and creaking as the house cooled from the heat of the day. Cicadas fiddling madly. A distant motorcycle revving.

Did she hear a noise coming from her bedroom? She held her breath until Edgar strolled out, and she laughed nervously. Rationally, she knew no one could be inside because the police had searched every inch of it. Still, she turned the television to a channel that played syndicated shows. She didn't want to hear the news. She also didn't want something to capture too much attention.

No, Jillian just needed background noise. A British woman was talking, and she glanced at the TV. Very nice. Jessica Fletcher would be good company while she reviewed the notebook from Stan's office.

Eventually, she closed it with a sigh. The information in the notebook matched what she had found on the thumb drive. She was relieved not to have possession of the data anymore. Maybe forensics could figure out more about a virus that would have disabled Stan's car. Apparently, cutting brake lines was too twentieth century for Stan's killer.

She went into her bedroom, lifted the mattress, and laid the notebook on the box springs. Then she changed into comfy pajama bottoms decorated with brightly colored cats and a green tank top. Her kitchen clock read 2:30, but she poured another cup of coffee and texted Allie.

--Still up?--

In less than a minute, her phone rang. "Of course. I don't think I'll sleep tonight."

"Me either. I read a notebook I found in Stan's office earlier. It summarized the same information I got off the thumb drive—Stan's client list, dollar amounts, and strings of numbers that probably tie to accounts."

"Dadgum. Jilly, I'm confused. How did someone know you had the thumb drive?"

"I don't know. Gayle's got it now. Only a few people knew I had it, and I trust all of them."

"And you're sure no one overheard you?"

181

"I can't imagine how." Jillian paused. "Unless…"

"Unless what?"

"We talked about the thumb drive when you were at the farmer's market, right?" Edgar jumped into Jillian's lap, and she held the little black cat close.

"I think so. Crabsticks! Do you think Betty overheard me?"

"It makes more sense than anything else. And she's always been the perfect accomplice for Stan."

"Yeah, but with the music, even I couldn't hear anything. I don't know how Betty could."

"Still, I'd better talk to Gayle tomorrow."

"Good idea. Are you okay there alone tonight? I could come over."

"Allie, I've got plenty of company—Edgar in my lap, you on the phone, and crime-solving Jessica Fletcher on the television."

Chapter Twenty-Nine

All night, Jillian heard sounds. Her rational brain knew she was safe, but her sense of violation was overwhelming. She tried to read her most recent mystery novel purchase, but after someone murdered a young woman in an empty house, she laid the book down with a shudder.

The sun finally began to glow through her closed blinds, and she gave up and crawled out of bed early. Edgar remained sprawled out, a black shadow on her sage-green sheets, unwilling to acknowledge the morning. She had repeatedly disrupted his beauty sleep with her tossing and turning, and he had some major napping to continue.

She made coffee and poured it into a travel mug to drink while she got ready and then take it with her. Today involved errands, not meetings, so Jillian chose jeans, chunky brown sandals, and a white sleeveless blouse. She ran a brush through her hair, pulled it back in a ponytail, and slicked on some lip gloss. She felt too tired for makeup.

Once she was ready, Jillian drove to the local electronics store and arrived while someone was flipping the sign to "open." She summarized her break-in without mentioning any details. The lanky salesman didn't appear over eighteen, and Jillian wondered if he understood alarm systems or if he had just scored a summer job. His slow words gave her confidence.

"Ma'am, you don't need to worry anymore. Once my guys get this system up and running, you can see your house from your phone whenever you want. Do you want us to include motion sensors?"

"I have a cat," Jillian explained. "Won't he set it off?"

"Prob'ly." The tall man smiled, showing crooked teeth. "Just don't let it scare you if you hear it. If it was me, I'd want to know, even if it was only a cat."

"Makes sense. When can you install it?"

"Usually, it takes us a couple of days, but we'll get it today," promised the man.

"Oh, that's great. So is this your store?"

Another display of teeth. "My dad opened it several years ago. Now that I'm out of high school, I work here during the day and go to the Vo-Tech at night. I'm Eddie, by the way."

"Eddie, you've been a lot of help, and I can't wait for you to install the system. Maybe I can sleep tonight."

He blushed. "That's what we try to do, ma'am."

"Please, Jillian." She extended her hand. "Nice to meet you, Eddie."

As she pulled out of the alarm store, she wanted to go back to bed, but she needed to stop by the chamber of commerce. She had promised to coordinate the equestrian portion of the surprisingly long 4th of July parade. Sometimes, it seemed more people participated than viewed it from the sidewalks.

This year's entries were impressive. The high school band would march, even though, unlike other parts of the country, school had dismissed for the summer in May.

The crowd always loved their annual rendition of "Stars and Stripes Forever." The floats also drew rave reviews. Every civic organization and church hooked a flatbed onto the back of a pickup, wrapped patriotic bunting on everything, and featured waving members. Sometimes, they even threw candy, much to the delight of the younger attendees. She hoped that Kiwanis reenacted the signing of the Declaration in a rough approximation of Trumball's painting. Brownies, dance groups, 4H, and utility companies would also participate, along with everyone's favorite, chugging antique tractors. The horses would end the parade immediately after the 4H kids and their cute livestock because no one ever wanted to follow animals.

She pulled up against the chamber of commerce's low, flat building, briefly closed her weary eyes, and sighed. Surely, the police could resolve everything in time for a fabulous 4th without fear that a murderer was running loose in Magnolia Hill.

She walked into the chamber's office and said hello to the staff working at desks in the lobby. Then she saw the president, Bob Wheeler, coming out of his office. "Hey, Jillian, are you checking on the equestrian entries?" he asked. Bob was on the upper end of middle age, his once-toned, high school football body now sporting rounded edges.

"We've got ten horses and riders registered so far. I expect more since we moved it to the morning. An evening parade might offer cooler temperatures, but we don't need early fireworks exploding and spooking the horses."

Bob nodded. "And it stretches the special events throughout the day and helps our restaurants get more foot traffic for lunch. Thanks for your help."

"I love Magnolia Hill's traditions," Jillian said. She left the chamber in a better mood than when she got there. She did love her town. Of course, she'd love it more if she found the money and Stan's killer was behind bars. And just that fast, her cheery mood faded again.

****

Jillian was ready for lunch when she pulled back into her garage. Thank God her front door remained closed, just like she'd left it. She entered the blessed air conditioning, and Edgar emerged from the bedroom, yawning and stretching in a way that suggested he'd caught up on his sleep.

"Hi, kitty. Rested?" He followed her to the kitchen, and she made a peanut butter sandwich on wheat and another pot of coffee. She loved Kandace's French press but also didn't mind plain, brewed java. It would help her stay awake. Edgar wrapped himself around her ankles until she got a can of food out of the cupboard hours before his dinner time.

After she ate her sandwich, Jillian knew she should get some work done, but she couldn't get motivated. Plus, the alarm installer would likely arrive soon. Instead, she decided to organize her clothing for the parade. She had participated in other 4th of July events and had plenty of choices. Before she could ride well, she had owned great Western clothes, boots, and hats.

She reached deep into the back section of her walk-in closet and found her red, white, and blue striped jeans and a royal blue shirt with fringe and sequins. She got a stepstool out and climbed up to reach a high shelf, clearing away some opportunistic spiderwebs. Edgar bounded up the steps beside her. She stretched her arms up and pulled down three boxes, hoping to find the hat she wanted. She hated being short!

The first box held the tie-dye hat, the second had flowers on the underside of the brim, but the third hit the jackpot. The final straw hat had a red crown with white stripes and a blue brim with stars. That would get the crowd's attention! She checked out her reflection in the mirror. She loved this hat and only got to wear it a few times a year.

After she organized her outfit and talked Edgar off the shelf with the promise of a treat, the security company arrived. Soon, Jillian could monitor every inch of her home at any time or place she wanted by using the phone app. The motion sensor had a sound alert, so she felt confident that nothing could happen without her knowledge.

After the installers left, Jillian released a deep breath, not realizing how frightened she had been. She went into the kitchen to figure out dinner. Nothing sounded interesting, so she ordered a combo pizza with extra jalapeños, even though she had eaten a couple of slices the night before. After it arrived, she collapsed onto the couch and clicked on the television. She watched mindlessly and ate, giving Edgar a few tastes. She might as well—if his other plans failed, the black floof would climb into the middle of her plate. Feeding him little bites created less mess and kept him out of her food.

Once Jillian and Edgar were satisfied, she stretched out on her couch and closed her eyes. She hadn't slept the night before and couldn't go any further without a short nap.

Chapter Thirty

The whistle of "The Good, The Bad, and the Ugly" woke Jillian. For a second, she was lost, not recognizing the familiar walls of her bedroom. Slowly, she realized she had slept on the couch, still wearing her clothes from yesterday. The morning news blared on the television, but it couldn't drown out her phone when the ringtone whistled again. Edgar yawned and curled tighter, displeased with the early morning. Wait, was it early? No, the horse clock in the kitchen proclaimed 8:00. She had slept almost twelve hours.

By the time she found her phone, the caller had hung up. She checked the ID, saw Will's name, and called him back.

"Hey, Jilly, did I wake you?"

She stretched her muscles, tight from sleeping in a ball, and tried to sound coherent. "Hi, Will. Uh, no. I was up." She knew her scratchy voice was betraying her.

"Did you sleep okay?" He seemed remarkably worried.

"I did. What's up?" She staggered to the kitchen, washed the pot from the night before, and started fresh coffee. She combed her hair with her hands and splashed water on her face.

"I just wanted to fill you in on the latest. Betty talked to the police about the guy who threatened Stan and later came into the office and yelled at her."

"You mean Derry?"

"Uh-huh. I thought I had met everyone in town, but I don't know him."

"Don't feel bad. I didn't either, so I went to his dry cleaners…"

"No surprise," laughed Will.

Jillian laughed even as she tried to remember she ought to be angry with him. "He moved back to town to live closer to his mother. She's friends with Penny and another victim of Stan's." She could tell by Will's silence that he was impressed. "You should know I don't give up until I find what I need," she continued.

"I'll keep that in mind. I wonder if the police believe Derry played a role in Stan's death," he mused.

"I would think so, but let me know if you learn anything," Jillian asked. "I know he looked furious at Stan's funeral, and then I overheard him threaten Betty in Stan's office."

Jillian could almost hear Will's mouth drop over the phone. "I suppose I shouldn't ask why you were hiding in Stan's office."

"Good," she replied. "You'll learn at some point that I have my methods."

She heard him laugh. "You may have sources, but I do, too, and I don't think you'll like what I've learned. I don't know if Derry killed Stan, but I know he didn't break into your house."

Jillian's heart sank. Derry made the perfect suspect because he had a motive, and she didn't like him. She didn't want the killer to be someone she had known her whole life. And she didn't want the killer to be Stan's hapless assistant. "How do you know?"

"I saw the pictures this morning for today's paper. The chamber of commerce reception and dinner started late afternoon the day before yesterday. I saw Derry in pictures taken throughout the event. If you heard the robber leave, the timelines don't work."

"Darn, I had intended to go to that, but with everything happening, I completely forgot. I hate that he has an alibi, not that I want him to have killed Stan," she added quickly.

"I know. And he still might have disabled the Porsche, but I think whoever broke into your house also murdered Stan."

"Yeah, I agree. So where does that leave us?"

"With one less suspect," offered Will practically. "There's something else I want to talk to you about, Jilly. Do you have any time later today?"

What could he want now? "A little this afternoon. I've got to get to the barn this morning. I can't believe the parade's only a few days away. Then I have some errands. But I should be finished by four."

"Could I buy you a coffee or a snack?" he asked.

"Sure. Do you want to meet at Peachy Pies?"

"See you then."

Jillian stared at the phone for several seconds after Will hung up. What did he want to talk about? She probably shouldn't have said yes to his offer, but she was curious, and she loved pie. Usually, she would have suggested Kandace's, but she didn't want to answer any questions later.

After she got off the phone, she threw on some barn clothes, anxious to get out to Agatha before the summer heat could build. Edgar finally got up and rubbed around her legs, reminding her he needed breakfast even if she hadn't gone to bed. She filled his bowl with dry food, and he glared at her indignantly. Kibble was not on his desired menu.

She patted his head, and his eyes closed. "Sorry, buddy. I'll get you something better later." She picked up Agatha's new saddle pad along with the patriotic medicine and overreach boots to protect and support the mare's lower legs. Then she grabbed more of the festive ribbon she had already shown Agatha.

She filled her travel mug with coffee and headed out. The peaceful drive in the soft morning light led to the ranch that spread across the bottomland outside of town. This part of the state typified how people imagined Oklahoma—wheat fields, pastures with horses, low scrubby trees lining the river at the back of the property, and the ability to see for miles and miles.

She opened her truck door and smelled freshly cut Bermuda grass. The maintenance guy must have recently mowed the outdoor turnouts. Beyond several pastures, she saw him still working on the other side of the ranch. He had probably started before dawn to finish before the blistering heat took over in the afternoon. Still, the temperature was surprisingly warm, and a plague of grackles lined up on the white metal fencing and complained about their situation. Jillian loved the descriptions of groups of animals. Anyone who had ever dealt with squawking, flocking grackles would know how they had earned the name "plague."

Agatha recognized her mom as Jillian walked down the aisle and nickered a "Good morning." Jillian yelled down the line of horses to her, and half a dozen of the ones she passed also nickered, "Hello." She mostly kept moving because if she talked to any of them too much,

Agatha would get jealous.

It was no surprise that by the time Jillian got to her run, Agatha had her ears pinned, and Mister gave her a side eye and plenty of room.

"Oh, Agatha, don't be a grouch." When she heard her name again, the mare's ears popped forward, and she walked up to Jillian.

The planner brushed the mare's red coat around her back and waist until the dust flew. She didn't want to put a saddle pad or a cinch over a burr.

Jillian knew red wasn't Agatha's best color, but that didn't matter when it was accompanied by royal blue and white. She braided the patriotic ribbons into Agatha's gray mane. When the wind caught them in the air, the horse calmly turned her head left and right to watch Jillian.

"Good job, Agatha." The horse nodded her head up and down. "Want to go ride?" She nodded again.

Jillian tacked her up with the beautiful rose-carved saddle and stood back to admire her four-legged friend. "Prettiest girl in the parade." Agatha nickered and shook her head up and down. Jillian laughed. Maybe the quarter horse felt agreeable, or maybe she had a fly tickling her ear.

After walking her to the arena, Jillian rechecked the cinch and tightened it by another hole. Then she swung her leg over and sat for a minute. With a cluck and gentle pressure, they stepped away. They walked, stopped, backed up a few steps, and then walked forward again. Eventually, they set off at a trot, and Agatha continued to ignore the ribbons.

Jillian knew many people didn't understand horses. Typical pets are predators; while dogs and cats hunt, horses do not. Horses don't chase their food. Instead, they are prey animals, and if frightened, they run to escape, using their legs for protection.

Jillian desensitized Agatha against her fear when Allie waved balloons, banners, and plastic bags. The friends also played loud music and unexpected noises. Over time, Agatha learned to trust Jillian and listen to her while no longer viewing distractions as threats.

They had done that work for years. Now, her mom just needed to remind Agatha that no matter what happened, she should listen to her. After a successful short ride, Jillian rinsed her down and tied her to the side of her run so she wouldn't roll in the dirt right after her bath. The planner sat on a hay bale and checked her phone while waiting for Agatha to dry. Then she fly-sprayed and untied her. After she reached for Agatha's cookies and got ready to leave, her life came flooding back. Who had sabotaged Stan's car?

Chapter Thirty-One

Jillian held cookies in her right hand, careful not to
drop the phone she also balanced. She questioned
Agatha. "If you wanted to sabotage a car, what would
you do to figure out how?" Agatha tapped Jillian's phone
with her nose, or maybe she wanted to get to the cookies.

"You'd use the phone?" Agatha shook her head no.
"Internet?" The horse's head bobbed up and down. "But
you wouldn't want to get caught, right?" she asked
Agatha. Her mare had an uncanny way of
communicating with her when she wanted to.

Agatha shook her head sideways, maybe to chase
away a fly, steal a cookie, or admit she wouldn't want to
get caught. Jillian glanced around, not wanting her barn
friends to overhear her or think she was crazy.

"How would you avoid it? I know. You'd go use a
computer somewhere else." Agatha nodded vigorously,
either agreeing with Jillian or emphasizing her love of
treats.

"If you wanted to hide your computer use, you'd
either destroy it or have an accomplice who could take
the blame," Jillian said triumphantly. Agatha held her
head up, made eye contact, and gazed expectantly like
she wanted Jillian to continue.

"Now Kandace's vandalism makes sense. I never
believed it sounded like random teenage destruction. I

need to talk to her again." Agatha took a deep breath, sighed, and dropped her head.

"Should I go now, or do you want me to brush you out first?" Agatha rubbed her face against Jillian's arm. "Okay, I've waited this long. I can wait another half hour." Jillian brushed the mare while Agatha's eyes slowly closed until she appeared to sleep. Helping solve a mystery had taken great energy.

****

By the time Jillian drove back to her house, bustle had replaced the stillness of the morning, and she had to wait at several lights before getting home. The longer she considered what she—and Agatha—had decided, the more she was convinced they were right. She couldn't wait to talk to Kandace.

Before she went to the coffee shop, though, she needed a quick shower to wash away the gritty red dust that stuck to her sweat. Even in the morning, she felt disgusting when she finished at the barn. But it could be worse. Summer weather was tough, but she hated the icy winter wind more and would rather be dirty than cold.

After her shower, Jillian slipped on white capris and a yellow sleeveless blouse. Flat sandals finished her outfit. She left her hair down and applied minimal mascara and lip gloss.

She called Allie on her way to pick her up. Her friend rocked shades of pink. Hot pink, pale pink, white, with surprising dashes of turquoise splotching her arms and legs. "I'm painting a crib today," Allie said excitedly. "I've created a little girl mermaid with a pink top and a shiny turquoise tail. I could have showered and changed with just a little warning," she reminded.

"Sorry," Jillian said. "I need to talk to Kandace, and

I want you to hear this."

"Did you figure something out?"

"Not completely. I hope you and Kandace will have some ideas."

As they approached Bits, Bytes, and Brews, Jillian could smell coffee before opening the door. She happily looked around at the new computer stations and minimalist tables with people working while sipping and munching. Kandace appeared to be operating at total capacity.

Soon, a cheery voice rose over the productive buzz. "Hey, friends, glad you stopped in. Do you want some coffee and something to eat?"

"I'd love an iced chai latte," Allie said.

"Sure," Jillian agreed. "You know I'll always take a coffee, and after parade practice with Agatha, I'm starving. Do you have a couple of minutes to talk?"

Kandace checked with the young assistant barista behind the counter, who nodded. "Sure, I've got some time. Where do you want to sit?"

"Could we go back to your office?"

Her friends appeared surprised. "Okay, but let's start with your order first," agreed Kandace. "What can we get you?"

"A large Peaberry, and do you have a sausage biscuit?"

"You've got it." The assistant nodded again.

Kandace motioned them to the back of the shop, and they went through a door sporting a shiny, new lock and entered her office right beside the elevator. Jillian believed the antique lift to be the coolest thing in the coffee shop. Made of open, massive wrought iron, it came up high enough on her waist not to scare her but still offered an open-air ride up and down. Watching the pulleys and cables fascinated her. In a murder mystery, Jillian would find the body sprawled on its floor.

For Kandace, the elevator provided critical access to her apartment upstairs. Much of downtown Magnolia Hill had undergone a "mixed-use" renovation, and Kandace's coffeehouse had been remodeled before she purchased the location. Trendy apartments now offered urban living above the merchant spaces below. Given the small-town vibe, Jillian wondered whether or not the planners knew the definition of "urban," but the units still provided a novel addition to the area.

Although most other shops had stairs, a wealthy owner of Kandace's space put in an elevator in the early twentieth century. The renovation team recognized the structure's historical value and saved it from demolition during the update.

Once the three women sat in Kandace's office, she directed a question at Jillian. "Okay, I'm intrigued. Why did we need to meet in here?"

"Hear me out. I believe someone specifically targeted your shop and destroyed it."

Allie's eyes got huge, and Kandace caught her breath before she tried to speak. "I told you, Jillian, that the police said random vandalism is on the rise, and the insurance company didn't open an investigation. And besides, Stan lost control of his car."

"But I've learned something else you don't know," Jillian said. Kandace's brown eyes narrowed, and Jillian continued, "Please don't repeat what I'm about to say because I can't prove it yet. If I'm right, you might not be safe, and you shouldn't involve anyone you don't know well."

"Less windup, more pitch," Kandace said. She tempered her critical words with a smile.

Jillian laughed. "Sorry. I want you to stay safe. Stan didn't just lose control of his car. Someone put a virus on his thumb drive that disabled it when it reached the ravine. He couldn't steer out of the way, and his car drove him over the cliff."

Kandace shuddered. "I didn't know you could put a virus on a car. If you're right, why hasn't Gayle told me this?"

"I might have known something I didn't share immediately with her," Jillian explained.

"You didn't tell the police anything until someone robbed you," Kandace guessed, and her friend nodded.

"Sometimes, you should be less of a crusader," Kandace scolded. "Why did the burglar think you had proof of what they did?"

"Because I had the thumb drive," she admitted.

"What? How? Never mind, I don't want to know." Jillian was getting used to that response. A knock at the door brought the assistant with the drinks and biscuit sandwich. She had also brought paper coasters and napkins, set everything up, and let herself out of the office.

After she left, Kandace continued. "You could have gotten yourself killed."

Jillian took a bite of the flaky biscuit and grilled sausage, sipped her coffee, and closed her eyes. "Thanks. You make the best coffee in town. All I thought I wanted was proof of Stan's cheating, not evidence of murder. I don't know how his killer knew I had it. I didn't tell anyone I don't trust."

Kandace got quiet for a minute, then raised her head.

"You think whoever disabled the car used the internet here to do their research?"

Jillian's shoulders softened when Kandace seemed to accept her theory.

"Oh man, how evil. Someone used my coffeehouse to commit a crime?" Her eyes filled with tears. Jillian knew Kandace loved her tough-as-nails persona, but inside, she also had a huge heart.

"You didn't know. And think of all the good you've done. I've seen you let people come in without ordering and use your computers for free when you knew they couldn't afford internet at home."

"I try," Kandace said. Her normally smooth face had deep lines of worry. "What do you think the killer did?"

"I think someone accessed the dark web from your computer. I suspect they even created a new email address that couldn't be traced back."

"Why would they do that?" Allie asked.

"I think they paid someone to create a virus that programmed Stan's car to lose control by the cliff."

"You can do that?" The color drained from Kandace's face.

"You can. Major car manufacturers have hired cybersecurity experts to keep entire makes and models of vehicles from being disabled."

"Seriously?" Allie said. "Why?"

"To extort money from the big car makers. Give us fifty million, or we'll stop every car of a certain make and model dead in its tracks. Cars would screech to a stop on highways, bridges, tunnels, and you name it. It would be a real-life disaster movie. Keeping ahead of these hackers is one of the most significant issues in automobile cybersecurity today."

"But the police never suggested anything like that to me," Kandace objected.

Jillian felt her face flush. "Well, I might have given them the idea. Will found a virus trail on the thumb drive."

"Will Anderson? I thought you guys didn't get along."

"We don't. It goes way back." Jillian hoped Kandace would let it go, but Allie seemed to enjoy tormenting her friend.

"Will wanted to save Jillian," Allie offered, grinning when Jillian glared at her.

"I didn't need saving."

"Of course, you didn't," Allie agreed, but she winked at Kandace while she did it. They both laughed, and Jillian glared again.

"Oh, calm down, Jilly." Allie sighed. "Everyone knows you can take care of yourself."

"And don't forget it," Jillian insisted. "Still, whatever I think of him, Will helped us figure out what had been installed on the drive. Not only that, he called this morning and said he had something he wanted to discuss."

Her friends both leaned into the table, and their mouths dropped. "What did you tell him?" Allie asked after a couple of seconds of silence.

"I asked if he wanted to meet at Peachy Pies. Don't even think of spying on us," she said, shaking her finger at them in mock anger. "I know too many people here," she explained to Kandace. "And I wasn't sure I wanted to tell you guys about it."

"Why not?" Allie asked.

"Because he probably just has a lead he didn't want

200

to discuss over the phone. I don't know. Something about his voice makes me think it might be more."

"Fill us in when you can," Kandace said. "In the meantime, maybe I can help with information about who used my computers. Remember, I told you I keep a list."

"What was stolen in the break-in?" Jillian asked, relieved not to be talking about Will.

"Only the last sheet. I keep the rest locked in this office in case something goes sideways."

"Do you mind if I see them now?" Jillian asked, around another bite of her crumbly biscuit and spicy sausage sandwich.

"No. Anyone can stop and look at the list because I keep it on the counter." Kandace rolled over to a filing cabinet and removed manilla folders labeled "May" and "June."

Jillian recognized most of the names on the sheets. "I didn't know how many people used your computers."

"It happens for various reasons—mostly just a desire to work in a room with other people. These days, folks seem to want company."

"Isn't that the truth?" Allie agreed. "Sometimes, I check my social media from here. I like the vibe."

Jillian turned the page. "Jeff Stone checked in ten days ago. Why was he here?"

"He said his laptop fried. I only saw him a few times."

"Derry Klingman signed in. I know he didn't break into my house, but I still don't trust him," Jillian admitted.

"Here's Betty's name, too. You're popular."

"We have big crowds," Kandace said. "I'm proud of what we built."

"You have every right," Jillian said as she kept reading names. "Even Stan was here."

"No, Stan drank coffee, but he always brought his own laptop," Kandace said.

"But his name is right here," Jillian insisted.

"I don't check the lists. I keep them if I need backup information about someone's laptop or illegal internet content. But I know who uses the computers. Trust me. Stan even told me that what he did was too important to put on a public computer. He never used one of my workstations."

"Even though I don't believe he cared, Stan's right about not using public computers. I can't either," admitted Jillian. "It's odd that his name is here."

"I understand that," Kandace agreed. "Now, Gina came in fairly often, but she worked alone."

"Yeah, I see her name, too."

"I know I can't prove he wasn't here, but I'm on the floor most of the time," Kandace said, "and Stan didn't work on my computers." She smoothed her black tunic top, almost like she was trying to soothe her frustration.

"I wonder who added Stan's name to the list?" Allie asked.

Jillian chewed and swallowed her last bite of biscuit. "I suspect whoever tampered with his car. If somehow a computer survived the vandalism and the police put everything together, they would think that Stan infected his own thumb drive. Whoever put together this scheme spent tons of time thinking it through."

She took a sip of coffee while she continued to review the list of suspects. "So many people could have been angry at Stan for stealing from them, even folks we don't know about yet. Losing your life savings or learning your parents were robbed could push a fragile person over the edge."

"Right," Kandace agreed. "We can't just run down all the citizens of Magnolia Hill. We need the name of the person who tore up my coffee shop."

"Maybe I can help with that. I know someone who's already trying to locate your vandals. He likes you a lot, but he had to gain the confidence of the people involved," Allie said to Kandace.

Jillian looked at Allie with respect. Her friend might come off as a flighty Bohemian, but she was always there in the clutch.

"Yeah, tell him I'd like to sleep again at night. If he cares about me, help me catch who did this."

"Let me see what I can do. I'll get back to you."

"Don't get into trouble," Jillian and Kandace said simultaneously.

"I won't be in any danger," Allie assured them. "And, Jilly, I expect a full report tonight about Will!"

"Let's get back out front," Kandace said. "I hate to leave the cafe for this long." They left her office, and Jillian stared at the elevator again.

Kandace noticed her expression. "Gorgeous, isn't it?"

"I love it."

"Yeah, me, too. People don't do that kind of craftsmanship anymore." Kandace turned around and headed toward the door. "Full report later, Jillian, and let me know if you find anything out, Allie. I hate everything about this."

Chapter Thirty-Two

Jillian's afternoon schedule hit a snag when she discovered nonpublic investments in a new client's portfolio. She hated securities that didn't trade on the open market, and by the time she found information on how he could sell them, it was almost four.

She wheeled under the faded pie sign at 4:05 and saw Will's Mustang of many colors parked in front. She gratefully entered the air conditioning and saw him slouching at a corner table. His face brightened a little when he saw her, and he motioned her over.

"I'm glad you could come. I always forget how much I like their pie."

Jillian glanced around to be sure she wouldn't be overheard. "I know it's a dive," she whispered, "but no one else makes a crust like this." She sat across the booth from him, and a cheerful, older server approached the table.

"Welcome, y'all. What can I getcha?"

Will encouraged Jillian to order first. "Do you have chocolate meringue?"

"I do, darlin'. Can I get you a slice?"

"Please, and a cup of coffee."

The server turned her attention to Will. "Same. I haven't had chocolate pie in years," he said.

"Well, you're in for a treat. Cream for the coffee?"

Jillian and Will declined, and the server closed her notebook and squeaked back to the kitchen. Maybe it was an employment requirement, thought Jillian. She searched briefly for the thin waitress from a few days ago but didn't see her. She hoped nothing had happened. The waitress returned with the coffee, and for a few minutes, Will said nothing. Jillian didn't know how to break the silence, so she waited.

Finally, he spoke. "I know you've been mad at me for a long time." He leaned back against the vinyl bench and ran his hands through his hair.

Woah, where was he going? Jillian thought he was going to talk about Stan, not her feelings about him. She needed something to do with her hands, so she added a little sugar to her coffee and stirred viciously. "We don't need to talk about it," she snapped.

"I think we do," Will disagreed. "You've been mad at me for fifteen years." When Jillian opened her mouth to speak, Will gently lifted a hand. "Jilly, it's a small town. You think I don't know you've been upset since our senior prom? I need a chance to try to clear my name."

"I think you're fifteen years too late for that," Jillian said stubbornly.

His features fell, and he flushed. "When I could, I tried to call Amber after that night. I did. But she wouldn't take my calls."

"You think I don't know that? I was there for most of them, trying to get her to stop crying. She answered one call if you remember."

The waitress returned with the two slices of pie. "Here you go. Let me know if I can get anything for you." The pie looked terrific, but the pain of the past destroyed Jillian's appetite.

Will sighed. "I remember. It was the worst day of my life. I asked her to understand, and she just hung up on me."

Jillian felt her old anger welling up until it spilled out her mouth. "Of course, she hung up on you! You stood her up the night of the prom. And then you ghosted her for days. When you finally got around to calling, you said, 'Please understand. It was important.' "

Will opened his mouth to speak, closed it, and then opened it again. "It was important," he said lamely.

"You know what was important?" Jillian spat out and then lowered her voice. She didn't want to be overheard, but no one was paying attention. "Amber thought you two would get married right after high school. She loved you. And you just blew her off and expected her to understand."

Will nodded miserably. "I know."

"I don't think you do," Jillian insisted. "She was so embarrassed about what you did that eventually, she and I drifted apart. She put space between herself and anyone aware of her breakup. I guess she wanted a fresh start. I tried to keep up with her, but eventually, I lost track. I have no idea where she is today."

"She's living outside Big Sky," Will said quietly.

"What? Do you mean that after all these years, you guys are in touch? And nobody bothered to tell me?" Hot tears rose in Jillian's eyes.

"No, no, no," Will said. "She has no idea that I know where she lives. It didn't seem fair. I just Googled her information about five years ago."

"So you're stalking her? That's much better," Jillian said sarcastically.

"No, Jillian, will you slow down for a minute?" Will begged. "I'm not stalking her, either. I just looked her up online. I have easier access to marriage records than you do. Her last name is Parker today. That's why you haven't been able to find her. She got married a couple of years after she left Magnolia Hill."

"She's married?" Jillian asked. "Good deal. I'm happy for her."

"Well, she was. She got divorced a few years ago. Maybe it was a rebound relationship, or something else went south."

"Well, if she married on a rebound, we all know whose fault that is." Jillian took a small bite of her pie, and the smooth chocolate was soothing.

Will sighed. "Yes, we do."

"So you know why I don't like you. It's even worse than that. I don't trust you, not that it makes any difference."

Will winced at Jillian's words. "It does make a difference, at least to me. I couldn't tell Amber what happened. You have to believe me when I tell you I couldn't help it."

"No, I don't. You could have always called or texted. She cried for days. What was so important that you just left her hanging?"

Will closed his eyes for a second, like he was debating whether or not he should tell his story. Finally, he opened them. "Do you remember my high school best friend, Josh?"

"Vaguely. Wasn't he that rich kid who got to miss the last two weeks of school because he had an internship in Europe or something?" Jillian remembered Josh thinking highly of himself.

"That's the story everyone told," agreed Will, "but it isn't true."

"What do you mean?" she asked and took another bite of the pie. Their conversation was exhausting.

"Even though prescription drug abuse is in the news now, it's always been an issue. Remember when Josh broke his leg in three places during the homecoming game?" Jillian nodded. "Well, he never got off the painkillers. When he couldn't get any more from his doctor, he bought them other ways. I was his friend, and I knew what he was doing, but I couldn't get him to stop. I figured his addiction would get better when he went away to college and had more to think about."

Jillian regarded him suspiciously. "You thought an addiction would get better on its own?"

"Hey, cut me some slack. I was an eighteen-year-old kid, and I didn't have anyone I could ask. I didn't want to get him in trouble. Anyway, on the day of the prom, Josh overdosed. He almost died. His mom called me that afternoon, and I drove like a maniac to the hospital. I blamed myself for not saying something to his parents."

Jillian was shocked. "How awful. I never heard anything about it. Why doesn't anybody know what he did?"

"Because, like you said, his parents had money. He went to the emergency room, but his parents moved him to a private hospital in Oklahoma City when he was stable. Once we knew he was okay, they sent him to rehab. That's where he was, not in Europe. He'd been to Europe before, so they had pictures. If you study his old social media closely, you'll notice he isn't in the same pictures as any famous landmarks. It was a giant scam."

"Why did it need to be such a secret?"

"Because his parents were afraid of what would happen if his college found out. Remember, he was headed back east to that ritzy school, and they didn't want him going in with the reputation of being an addict."

Jillian shook her head in disbelief, and Will seemed relieved to stop talking for a minute. He forked a bite of pie and drank his coffee deeply. On cue, the waitress appeared to refill their cups.

"Why couldn't you tell Amber?" Jillian asked.

"His parents forbid me to tell anyone. His dad threatened that if I told, he would float rumors about me with potential employers."

"What a jerk!" Jillian said.

Will nodded sadly. "I know he cost me one job while I was in college, even though I kept their secret. I had an interview, and everything seemed great, but they called me back. They said they had discovered discrepancies in my records and couldn't hire me. I think his dad sabotaged me to prove he could."

"Is that why you're at the paper?"

"Don't get me wrong. I love being a reporter, but I had bigger aspirations than *The Magnolia Daily*. Eventually, I told my dad what happened, and he thought it might be easier for me to get a job where no one would question my credentials. And I've come to love it over the last fifteen years."

Jillian's head was whirling with all the information. Everything she believed about Will was wrong. Of course, he shouldn't have abandoned Amber, but he was in a bad spot. And Josh's controlling father was the problem, not Will's dad.

"Wow. I'm sorry. I feel bad for you, Amber, and

even Josh. I haven't heard anything about him in a long time. Do you know where he is?"

"He's in Dallas. His dad bought his way through college and law school, and even though he went through rehab, he still has issues. We don't stay in touch, but mutual friends tell me he's had a couple of DUIs and still parties way too hard. He never paid any consequences, so he thinks he's above it all. I'm afraid I'll get a bad phone call someday." Will set down his coffee cup and stared at his plate, searching back through the years.

"I hate all of this," Jillian said. "Everybody got hurt. I can't believe you never told Amber after all these years."

"How could I? Once I let it go too far, I couldn't very well call her and tell her what I'd done years earlier. Plus, I don't want to date her now. Too many years…too much pain…we're different people now."

"I get that, but even if you never see her, you should tell her what happened. It will silence that tiny voice in her head that she did something wrong."

"Oh, gosh, no. None of this was her fault." Will ran his hand through his hair again, and Jillian could feel the table jiggle as his knee bounced up and down.

"She doesn't know that," she insisted.

"Okay, I'll give her a call. You're right. It's the only fair thing to do. I have her number, but I don't know how to start." Will sounded sad and frustrated.

Jillian offered encouragement. "I think the way you told me worked just fine. You might try something like this. Buy her some pie."

"I will. I couldn't leave you thinking I was a jerk who blew off your friend. I don't blame you for being angry with me."

"I'm glad you told me," Jillian said. "But why now?"

"I didn't care until the night of your robbery. I realized I want you to be safe, and I want you to trust me. You can't trust me without knowing the truth."

"No," she agreed, "I can't. But it took a lot of courage to own up to something that happened so many years ago. You could have let it go. I think telling Amber will help you get real closure, yourself. It sounds like you deserve it."

Jillian walked out of the restaurant feeling like the weight of all those years had been released. Of course, Will should have told Amber, but he was a victim, too. She wished his father would have intervened, but she also recognized that the Andersons didn't earn much money in small-town journalism. At least not compared to Josh's family. She suspected the father's guilt over being able to do nothing for his son had led to some of his critical nature. It was easier to blame Will than own what he couldn't fix.

After she sat in her truck and turned on the AC, she reached for her phone. She had to call Allie. Then she paused. Will had taken her into his confidence, and he needed to talk to Amber before she heard the story somewhere else. That would make a terrible situation even worse. She'd tell her friends, and maybe even her parents, but only after Will let her know he had tried to make amends. As she started to back out of the gravel lot, she turned on her radio and sang along to "Party in the USA" with Miley Cyrus.

Chapter Thirty-Three

Jillian didn't get home from her office the next day until late afternoon. Part-time sleuthing took time she needed to spend on her business, and she had spent the day focused on unfinished tasks and reports. She changed from a denim skirt, red blouse, and red heels into floral shorts, a pink top, and sneakers. She pulled her hair into a ponytail, wandered into the kitchen, and searched for something to eat. Edgar followed her, meowing pitifully, when she put on a pot of coffee. He barely had his wet food when she heard a knock at her door.

After the burglary, she appreciated Allie's heads-up that she would stop by. She hadn't offered why she wanted to come but often dropped in, so Jillian hadn't asked any questions.

Checking through her peephole, she saw that Allie had company. The tall, slim man had jet-black hair and the hint of a tattoo at the neckline of a crisp, white shirt. Then Jillian noticed his eyes—pale blue with black lashes. She only knew one person who had eyes like that. Ace. She opened the door.

"Allie, Ace, welcome!" She shot Allie a questioning look, and Allie ignored her. "I just put on a pot of coffee. You guys want some?"

"Always," Allie said.

"Same," Ace said. "I never turn down coffee."

"You're in good company here. I'll bring it out. Have a seat anywhere." When they sat, Jillian was surprised that they chose the same loveseat rather than sitting in separate chairs. What was going on? She got out a tray and added three mugs, cream, sugar, spoons, and the pot. Then she carefully carried it to her appropriately named coffee table and set it beside the latest political thriller she was reading. Edgar followed her and immediately jumped in Ace's lap. The lanky man stroked him absently. Jillian always trusted the people that Edgar liked.

"Ace, it's good to see you again finally. I hear you went into accounting."

"Who would have ever believed that?" Ace had the easy laugh of someone who didn't take himself too seriously. "After my years in the band, reveling as a free spirit, now I crunch numbers. But I'm good. I've been a CPA for several years and have my own practice."

"More power to you," Jillian said appreciatively. "Running your own business has challenges."

"No kidding. But I came over because Allie asked me for a favor." Allie smiled at him more brightly than she did at Jillian. She swept her hair back with a turquoise-stained hand. She must still be painting the crib.

"Do you remember that I thought I could help us figure out who vandalized Kandace's coffeehouse?" Allie said. "Well, Ace volunteers to tutor high school kids having trouble in math."

"I bet you're good at that," Jillian said.

"Not bad." Ace ducked his head. Jillian didn't remember him being shy. "I figure if I could turn into a

STEM person, anyone could. I can talk to the kids from a position of not being a great high school student."

"Anyway," Allie continued, "he found out some of his students might have vandalized Kandace's place, and he wants to help them find a way out."

Jillian stared at Ace in amazement. "Do you know who destroyed the coffee shop?"

Ace looked uncomfortable. "I don't know anything for sure. The kids didn't want to talk to me about it. But I think so. I've heard rumors that their behavior is more complicated than it appears. They're not bad kids. They just got caught up in a tricky situation."

"But Kandace's vandalism seems like a lot more than normal troublemaking." Jillian had no sympathy for anyone who mistreated Kandace.

"Yes, but they aren't the vandals who spray graffiti everywhere. They're normally good kids, I promise. I told them they had to come clean, but I would be supportive."

"What did they tell you?"

"The group told me a hypothetical story. They didn't outright admit to it, but they were transparent. I mean, they're teenagers, not hardened criminals. They're easy to read. I want them to make things right, and they've begged me not to go to the police." He held out both hands apologetically.

"Okay," Jillian said slowly.

"I didn't know their behavior might relate to something bigger until Allie told me about the situation with Stan. If I had any idea things were this serious, I'd have gotten firm with them sooner. I wanted them to come to the right decision, themselves. But after everything Allie told me, I want the group leader, Lucas, to talk directly to Kandace. I think he should explain what happened. Plus, I want him to take responsibility for what he's done. I'd love it if you came with us."

"I wouldn't miss it," said Jillian. She glanced at Allie, who still stared at Ace. "Allie?"

Her friend's pale skin flushed to bright pink. "I wouldn't miss it either."

"I think we should do it now," Ace said. "You guys okay with that? I may need to give him a ride. Can you, two, ride together without getting into more trouble?" Allie and Jillian laughed.

"Maybe," they said together.

Chapter Thirty-Four

On the ride to Kandace's, Jillian called her to see if she could talk. She heard her call out to an employee who offered a muffled response.

"Of course. Come on in. I'll get you guys some coffee," Kandace said.

Once she hung up, Jillian glanced over at Allie, who sat staring out the window, uncharacteristically quiet.

"How long have you been seeing Ace? And why didn't you tell me?" she asked her friend. She worked hard not to think that she was also withholding information about Will. She guessed everyone had their secrets.

Allie studied the blue paint on her nails. "I wouldn't call it dating, really," she said. "We hang out a little. I didn't want to say anything to you because I needed to decide how I felt about it. You know, I broke up with Ace."

"I remember. You wanted to go to college, and Ace wanted to get married. You thought you should wait." Jillian didn't mention it, but she also remembered talking to Ace and Allie, individually, and they told her how much they loved each other.

"I did, and I still think I made the right decision even though I cried for weeks. I wasn't ready to get serious then. Geez, maybe I'm not now."

"Take it slow," encouraged her friend. "You know, I always liked Ace."

"I did, too," Allie said. "I still do. And I love the work he does with these kids. They don't have anyone they can trust, let alone encourage them to try to excel."

"I'm glad he convinced Lucas to talk to Kandace. Maybe some of the mystery will make sense," Jillian said.

"He knows that. He doesn't want to scare them off. He's worked hard to win their trust. But when I told him what we'd learned about Stan's fraud and suspicious death, he knew he had to get more firm with them. I want this to turn out well, and I know Ace does, too."

Jillian and Kandace entered the cheerful coffee shop for the second time in two days.

Kandace rolled up with a small tray holding two cups, one for a hot beverage and one for an iced. "What's going on?"

Jillian gestured toward a corner table away from other patrons. "Let's grab a table."

"Ace should get here soon," Allie added.

"Ace?" Kandace sounded surprised. "What does he have to do with anything? He didn't vandalize my store."

"No," Allie said, "but he thinks he knows who did. He's bringing him here today."

Almost on cue, the door opened, and Ace walked in with an older teen displaying a defiant expression. Ace motioned him over to the table, and they sat down beside each other, with Ace's companion leaving two empty chairs between Jillian and him.

He had several piercings in each ear and one on the side of his nose. A short-sleeved tattoo extended below his T-shirt on his left arm. His long hair had a green

217

streak. However, unlike Allie's brightly colored spikes, this young man's demeanor made the stripe seem sinister and angry. But then she noticed his frightened expression.

Ace took a sip of water from a glass one of the servers provided. "Kandace, meet Lucas. Lucas led the group that vandalized your coffee shop. He agreed to talk to you, knowing you can call the police whenever you want."

Lucas stared hard at the slate gray Formica tabletop, and for a moment, no one spoke. Then Kandace cleared her throat.

"Hi, Lucas. I'm Kandace, and I own this shop. Why were you so angry at me that you wrecked it?" Her voice was level and low without a trace of judgment.

Again, no one said a word. Ace focused on Lucas until he finally made eye contact. Lucas fidgeted uncomfortably like he wanted to bolt, but he finally nodded at Ace.

"I'm sorry, Kandace. You didn't do anything to my friends or me. Someone offered us money to trash your store." He twisted and untwisted his napkin with his hands.

"Offered you money?" Kandace's voice caught on the words. "Who would do something like that?"

Lucas seemed even more miserable. "I don't know. Honest. She paid us cash."

"Us?"

"The guys I hang with. She paid us each 500. She told us we needed to tear up the computers and make the rest look like vandalism. We acted like idiots and didn't think about the effect on you. All we could see was the money. My family doesn't have a lot at home..." His voice trailed off.

"That amount must have seemed enormous to you," Kandace said, holding her tone even, and Lucas nodded.

"I hope the money will be worth it when you have to explain what you did to the police," Jillian said. Lucas appeared to be sixteen or seventeen—old enough to know better, in her opinion.

He started to speak, but Kandace interrupted him. "Lucas, I haven't said I would call the police."

"What?" Jillian, Allie, and Ace screeched simultaneously. Lucas finally looked up at Kandace, not saying a word.

"Oh, I'm not promising that I won't," she continued quietly, "but I want to hear who offered Lucas so much money that he destroyed my coffee shop."

"Ma'am. I don't know her," Lucas said in a voice less hostile. A glimmer of hope shone in his eye.

"I'd much rather you call me Kandace than ma'am, okay? I'm not that old." She smiled, and Lucas seemed to relax a little.

"Okay. Can you describe this woman?" Kandace asked.

"She had brownish blonde hair, not much makeup, and she seemed frightened. She didn't stand up straight and dressed like an old woman."

Jillian glanced around at the group, knowing that "old" to a teen didn't mean geriatric. "Betty?"

Chapter Thirty-Five

Jillian stared at Lucas in amazement, then back at her friends. Again, no one said anything for a moment. Finally, Allie gulped a breath and spoke.

"Betty must have heard me at the farmer's market! I didn't think I was that loud."

Jillian patted her friend's arm in sympathy. "I'm louder than you, but Betty might have overheard you. Remember, you said she was staring at you."

"You know, that night, I thought she was afraid." Sitting at the chrome table, Allie looked frightened, herself, while Ace sat with his head in one of his hands, his white shirt pulled up on his arm, showing a tattoo. Kandace rolled back and forth slowly, a move she made when thinking hard. Lucas seemed confused, but at least his face had lost the surly expression he wore when he entered the store.

Jillian's mind whirled. Betty had always been the most logical choice for the murderer. Still, her denial had been fierce. She must have better acting skills than she would have expected.

Kandace's voice interrupted Jillian's judgment. "Lucas, I need to call Officer Gayle Johnson, but I don't intend to get you in trouble. I do, however, want Betty arrested. Before I accuse her of something she might not have done, please describe her one more time. Can you remember any other details?"

The teen closed his eyes and replayed the scene. "We were hanging out in the alley behind the grocery store when she drove up and got out of her car."

"What kind of car?" interrupted Ace.

"A white Ford," Lucas said, and Jillian nodded. She'd seen a white Ford parked in front of Stan's office.

"She asked us if we wanted to earn some easy money. She flashed a big wad of bills and said she'd give us 500 apiece after we vandalized the shop. She told us she'd meet us back there in the alley."

There was more to Betty than met the eye, thought Jillian. "Okay, Lucas, what else?"

Lucas closed his eyes again. "Brownish blonde hair cut in layers—badly—maybe she cut it herself. She wore a long-sleeved white blouse and short black pants, and I don't mean skinny pants. Like they had shrunk. Boring shoes, worn black loafers. Nothing seemed expensive. Medium-length nails with reddish-brown polish. Almost no makeup. Just super average."

"Good details," Jillian praised, and he blushed.

"Thanks for your help," Kandace said. Everyone smiled at the teen, who seemed relieved after finally telling the truth.

Jillian agreed with Ace. Lucas was headed in the wrong direction but wasn't a bad kid.

"Did you get everything repaired?" Lucas glanced around. "It looks nice."

Kandace surveyed the repairs proudly. "I did. I had good insurance."

"Are you gonna tell the cops about me?"

"Not now. We need to deal with what you told us first. But I might want to work out a repayment program directly with you. Sending you to jail would make me sad and ruin your life. I know a little bit about that."

Tears formed in the corners of Lucas' eyes just for a second. He wiped his face roughly, and then he spoke to Kandace. "I'd do anything to make this right."

"We'll talk more later," she promised.

Jillian glanced down at her phone. "Y'all, I'm sorry. I've got a client meeting in thirty minutes. Allie, can you get a ride with Ace?"

Ace and Allie both grinned at each other. "Sure," she said.

"No problem," he agreed. Jillian slipped away from the table and walked quickly to her truck.

****

Once behind the wheel, she worked to catch her breath and process what Lucas had said. Someone had dressed like Betty to frame her, but the woman who offered the money wasn't Stan's assistant. However, Jillian knew the killer's identity and turned her truck to Stan's house.

Stan lived in a wealthy part of Magnolia Hill. Once she arrived at his drive, she wondered if she was making a mistake. How would Gina handle the confrontation? At the last second, she sent a text message to Allie, telling her what she believed. Someone needed to know her location.

Jillian knocked on the door with a shaky hand, and her stomach flipped when Gina answered.

The glamorous blonde seemed older and less impressive without her makeup and designer clothes. When she saw Jillian, she glared for a moment before she caught herself.

"Jillian. What a surprise. What can I do for you?"

Jillian's heart pounded so hard she saw her shirt moving. Why had she come here? Why hadn't she just given the information to Gayle? She answered her own question. Because Jeff wouldn't agree to question Gina. It took more than a manicure to convict someone of murder.

"Hi, Gina. I was driving through the neighborhood and wanted to stop and ask you a couple of questions about Stan's death."

Gina waved her inside. The stylish woman's influence didn't appear to shape the decor. Stan's family room was a large, expensive man cave with brown leather furniture and a mahogany cart filled with crystal decanters of bronze liquid, likely his favorite bourbon. A giant state-of-the-art television filled an entire wall, and the whispered scent of cigar smoke reminded her of a sad incense. Jillian cautiously sat on a stool beside the cart.

"What do you need?" Gina perched on the edge of a sectional couch.

Jillian took a deep breath and plunged in. "Why did you pay Lucas and the other teenagers to trash Kandace's coffeehouse?"

Just for a second, Gina blanched, and Jillian knew she was correct. The knowledge provided absolutely no comfort or sense of accomplishment.

Gina recovered quickly. "I don't know what you're talking about."

"Sure, you do. You dressed like Betty, even rented a car like hers, and paid the teens enough to guarantee they would destroy the computers."

"I didn't do that," Gina hissed.

Jillian shook her head sadly. "You did. You almost captured Betty's appearance, but your manicure gave you away. She bites her nails, and you don't. Her hands look ragged, and yours always match your outfit."

At the accusation, Gina's face twisted in rage. "You're crazy. Why would I pay teenagers to destroy the computers?"

Jillian hoped the ping she heard on her phone was Allie acknowledging her message. "Because you didn't want anyone to find the virus you installed on Stan's thumb drive. You used Kandace's computers to pay someone on the dark web to develop a virus that would activate when Stan updated his car." Jillian's words tumbled over each other, and the horror of her accusation registered in her voice and on Gina's face.

"How dare you? Why would you sit around and create lies about me?"

"You know I'm not lying. You created a plan to kill Stan when the virus disabled his Porsche. He couldn't steer, and you knew the wreck would send the car over the cliff. I just don't understand why you did it."

Gina reached into the end table drawer beside her and pulled out a gun. "You've always acted like you're more virtuous than all of us. You caused his death."

Jillian's legs felt like they wouldn't hold her up, even if she dared to stand. Despite the air conditioning, she began to sweat. And worst of all, she didn't know what Gina meant.

"What are you talking about?"

"I guess you made him feel guilty, and he lost his nerve. He told me he didn't want to retire on the money we had stolen." Gina's cold, hard voice ended in a joyless laugh. "He developed a conscience and told me he wanted the respect you had in town."

"But everyone loved him," Jillian protested.

"They did, but he knew he didn't deserve it, and he hated that. After everything I had organized, he was going to turn us in and give the money back! We had enough to live in luxury in Central America. And he was going to give the money back and ruin everything." Gina's laughter grew more and more manic, and the hair on the back of Jillian's neck stood straight up.

"I paid for the virus and then waited, hoping he would come to his senses. Bad luck for him that he didn't. You told him you knew he was a phony during your fight at Kandace's. After you left, he told me he couldn't be part of the fraud any longer. He tried to talk me into returning the money, and I knew he no longer fit my plan."

"So, you killed him before he could do the right thing," Jillian said in horror.

"I tried, but I was only half successful. Stan didn't get a chance to give anything back, but when I checked our bank account after his tragic accident, it was empty. The money's gone. All of it."

Jillian figured that the longer she could keep Gina talking, the more likely Allie would send help. "Everything? Where did he move it to?"

Gina snarled. "If I knew, it wouldn't be gone. Stan always admired you. I meant it when I told you that on the day of his funeral. You thought I meant it as a compliment, but I didn't. Stan was weak, and your 'saved my grandmother' virtue always triggered his guilt." She raised the gun, and Jillian fought for something to say.

"You don't want to do this."

"Why would I care about killing you? I already killed Stan. I know you didn't tell anyone what you suspected because even a bad friend would talk you out of coming here and confronting me. I'll give you credit—you've got nerve, not that it will help you. Once you're dead, I'll dress back up like Betty and make sure someone sees her dragging something large into the woods. By the time the police figure out she didn't do it, if they ever do, I'll be gone. I may not have the money, but I won't go to prison."

She raised the gun, and Jillian squeezed her eyes shut in anticipation of the shot. Suddenly, pounding at the door made them both jump. "Police!" Gayle screamed. Gina froze for a second, and Jillian saw her opportunity and lunged behind the cart. When Gina turned back toward her, Jillian threw one of the decanters. Bronze liquid swirled through the air as the crystal made contact with Gina's shoulder. As she fell, she wildly fired the gun toward the ceiling, and the sound was enough for Gayle to break down the door.

Chapter Thirty-Six

Still behind the cart, Jillian stared as Jeff and Gayle ran in screaming, "Put the gun down." The officers stopped in amazement when they saw Gina lying on the floor, covered in bourbon, holding her arm.

Once Jeff led Gina to the police car, Jillian took Gayle's arm gratefully, since her legs still threatened to buckle. Gina sat in the back of the cruiser glaring at them. Even though she knew Stan's wife wasn't a threat anymore, the rage in her eyes still made Jillian's blood run cold.

"Thank God Allie got my message," Jillian finally said. Once the police broke down the door, Gina dropped her gun and put her hands over her head. She couldn't overpower half of Magnolia Hill's police force.

"Girl, you are lucky," Gayle said. "Allie called us, and we got here as fast as we could. Tell me again how you knew the killer was Gina and not Betty. And maybe also explain how you could be so stupid that you decided to confront her yourself?"

Jillian sat on the curb's edge, and Gayle plopped down beside her. Although the officer tried to sound critical, the relief in her voice was unmistakable. Before Jillian could say anything, Allie's Prius and Penny's convertible tore up the street. They raced out of their cars while Ace and Will helped Kandace get her chair out of

Allie's trunk. Then they all enveloped both Jillian and Gayle in a giant hug.

Penny saw Jeff standing to the side, and much to his horror, she hugged him, too. He pulled back, she laughed, said something, and finally got a hug out of the grumpy officer.

"Okay, gather round," Gayle said. "Master sleuth, here, wants to explain how she figured out the killer was Gina."

Half a dozen sets of questioning eyes focused on Jillian. "It was the manicure," she said simply. "I've spent a lot of time with Betty lately, and she bites her nails down to the quick, bloody levels of biting. She would never think to wear fake nails. Remember, Kandace? You told me Gina liked her manicure to match her outfit. She probably never thought about Betty's hands."

Jillian put her arm around Allie, whose red eyes threatened more tears. "You figured it out first."

"I did?" Allie asked incredulously.

"Remember the stain on the thumb drive?"

"The blood?"

"Except it wasn't blood. Nail polish made the stain, although I would have never figured that out if Gina hadn't slipped up on her imitation of Betty."

Jillian and Gayle filled in the rest of the details, and Penny shook her head sadly and tsked. "Poor Stan. Killed for finally developing a conscience."

"I wonder where the money is," Kandace said.

"I think we found the account. Remember that file that only had the string of numbers?" Jillian reminded. She motioned to Gayle. "Y'all can locate the bank."

"About time," Gayle said. "Please let us do our job."

"Amen," Penny said.

Jillian got up and walked over to Will. "How did you find out about this?"

Will looked at Allie and said, "The press has its sources." He put his arm tight around Jillian's shoulders. Jillian hated to admit the feeling didn't leave her repulsed. "Next time, call me," he whispered.

"Next time," Allie screeched. "There better not be a next time."

****

The following day, the 4th of July, dawned bright and clear. Jillian had never made it to the barn the night before, so she got up at dawn and went out to the ranch. Right after Agatha ate her breakfast, Jillian gave her a good scrubbing, made easier because Agatha liked baths.

Once the mare dried, Jillian put her in the trailer and organized all their 4th of July tack and accessories. Then she drove the trailer to the gathering point. After all the rain, she was happy to see a sunny day for the parade, even if it would lead to a hot afternoon. After yesterday, she was fortunate to see it at all. She couldn't think about Gina for too long, or she felt sick. At least Stan's killer was finally behind bars.

Jillian tacked up Agatha with her red, white, and blue saddle pad and rose-tooled leather saddle. She picked out her feet and noticed the sparkly polish.

"The other day, you kept stamping your feet to tell me about the nail polish, didn't you, pretty girl?" Agatha nodded, or maybe she was only rubbing her nose on Jillian's back. Jillian laughed while she wrapped on the mare's patriotic medicine and overreach boots with stars. Finally, she braided Agatha's mane with red, white, and blue ribbons.

She finished the last streamer, and Betty walked up beside the trailer. "Jillian, I just wanted to say thank you. You kept me from facing a murder trial."

"At least we got it figured out," Jillian said, offering the mousy woman a hug. Betty accepted it gratefully. "I've got a question, though. Did you see Allie at the farmer's market in Big Sky?"

"I did. Your friend was standing right in front of Gina."

"So you were staring at Gina, not Allie."

"Why would I stare at Allie?" Betty asked, confused.

"Well, now that I understand everything, you weren't. But I bet Gina could overhear what Allie said to me."

"I'm sure." Betty nodded. "Anyway, I know you're busy. I just had to say thank you."

"What will you do now?" Jillian asked.

"I'm going to leave Magnolia Hill. My brother works for a company near Tulsa, and they need an administrative assistant, a real one that does actual work. I've taken the job."

"You'll like that better, I think. Good luck!" She watched the woman walk away and hoped her new life would lead her to better things.

Once Betty was gone, Jillian entered the small living area at the front of the trailer. She changed from cut-offs and a tank top to the red, white, and blue outfit she had picked out earlier. Wow, what a long few days!

Still, the outcome reminded Jillian of Penny's old Polish phrase, "Things will work out in the end." That morning, news reporters announced that after working all night, the police had found Stan's new bank account.

Remarkably, out of the twelve million dollars Stan had managed to con out of the citizens of Magnolia Hill, they had recovered everything but $200,000, great news compared to the disaster that usually ended these stories.

She was almost dressed when her cell phone rang. Nancy sounded joyful on the other end of the call. "Have you heard the news? They found my money, or at least nearly all of it. I'm going to be okay."

"Yes, you are. I'm so happy that the funds aren't gone," Jillian agreed.

"I just can't believe Stan's wife killed him. Some people are good at disguising their feelings."

"Yes, they find a way to hide it behind a lot of polish," Jillian said, laughing at her own joke. After they hung up, Jillian realized that Gina was right. She cared about her clients as much as she had worried about her grandmother's money, although she didn't intend to risk death for them again.

Now fully dressed and with her favorite red, white, and blue cowboy hat on her head, she swung her leg up over the back of Agatha and got in formation with the rest of the riding group. She could hear the bands already playing in the distance. The parade had started.

Agatha and Jillian started to walk down the parade route. Allie and Penny waved wildly at her, and she waved back. Will stood behind them, and when he tipped his ball cap at her, she smiled.

Recipes for Financial Success

Recognizing Ponzi Schemes

Jillian was surprised Penny knew that a Ponzi scheme involves a con posing as a financial professional who takes your funds with the promise of investing them. Unfortunately, the funds aren't actually deposited in your account. Instead, the con has cashed the check and is spending your money.

If you need to receive money from your account, the con has to find a new "investor" and give you their money for your distribution. Ponzi schemes usually fall apart when too many people want their money at the same time.

Jillian recognized Stan's Ponzi scheme because his actions exhibited common characteristics of financial fraud. Here are some red flags that Jillian thinks investors should investigate.

Investment returns are consistently positive, even in down markets. We all know that the stock market goes up and down. If your investments only earn positive returns, ask questions. Jillian wishes that her clients always made money, but she knows that portfolio declines are part of investing.

The financial professional delays requests for distributions. Investment accounts shouldn't be revolving doors for cash flow. However, if one of Jillian's clients needs money from an account, she acts promptly and doesn't pressure them to leave it invested.

The financial professional keeps custody of the money. Most financial professionals hold, or custody, their clients' portfolios at reputable custodians or brokers. Jillian worried when she couldn't find the name of the custodian on Stan's investment statement. One way a certain infamous financial criminal hid his theft was by claiming he custodied his clients' money, himself. If you have concerns, call the custodian/broker-dealer phone number on your statement, and confirm you have an account there.

The financial professional has the client write funding checks payable to the professional. When money is deposited in an investment account, the check is payable to the custodian, not the financial professional. When Jillian's clients open accounts, they don't write their investment deposits payable to her. They make them payable to her custodian.

Investments are opaque and difficult to research. Although everyone has different goals and risk tolerance profiles, Jillian prefers to invest in publicly traded securities that can be researched. When investments don't trade on the stock market, it can be difficult to find information about them or determine their price. The lack of transparency makes it tricky to know how much money is in the investment.

Questions to Ask a Financial Professional

Jillian always welcomes questions from potential clients before they begin to work with her. Although she knows each new client may have different needs and expectations, basic information can eliminate confusion later, and she wants them to understand how she does business. Here are some of the most important questions she wants to address.

What services do you provide? Jillian is a CERTIFIED FINANCIAL PLANNER^{TM} practitioner, so she provides financial planning in addition to investment services. She helps clients save for retirement, minimize their taxes, manage their cash flow, evaluate their insurance, and many other topics. Additionally, she helps clients create investment portfolios that match their risk tolerance and help them meet their goals. Some financial professionals only provide investment services, and some only do planning. She believes you should understand the scope of services your financial professional provides.

How are you compensated? Everyone gets paid, but some types of compensation are more difficult to recognize than others. Whether you are paying fees or commissions, you should know how much your financial professional is receiving. Sometimes, to understand the level of compensation, Jillian suggests that a client ask how much the professional is getting from any source for the implementation of a strategy. She hopes the professional will disclose money paid both by the client and the product provider.

How often will we meet? The number of meetings per year and the method of communication should be established early. Some of Jillian's clients want to meet with her twice a year in person, while others prefer an annual phone call. In any case, she helps them understand the meeting schedule after she has completed initial implementation of her services.

Can you explain your investment strategy or how you select any investment managers you use? Jillian wants to explain her decision-making process to her clients. She knows financial professionals can have different beliefs, and she thinks it's important that they explain them to their clients. If the financial professional uses a different, or third-party, portfolio manager, she thinks the professional should understand their methods and be able to summarize them.

Are you willing to be my fiduciary? The fiduciary standard has been a contentious issue for several years. Being a fiduciary is a legal status, and it involves making decisions for clients without regard to any personal gain. For example, an investment should be chosen because the professional believes it is the best, not because he or she is receiving extra compensation for recommending it. Jillian believes it's important for everyone in financial services to be willing to provide a fiduciary level of care.

For additional questions, Jillian refers prospective clients to the CFP® website, www.letsmakeaplan.org, where they can find a more exhaustive list to ask when interviewing potential professionals.

A word about the author…

Best-selling personal finance author Peggy Doviak started reading the Bobbsey Twins when she was a child. Now, an experienced financial planner who changed careers when a stockbroker exploited her mother, she is realizing her dream of publishing a cozy mystery series. If bakers can solve murders, why can't financial planners? Peggy lives in Oklahoma and is owned by two cats and two horses.

Thank you for purchasing
this publication of The Wild Rose Press, Inc.

For questions or more information
contact us at
info@thewildrosepress.com.

The Wild Rose Press, Inc.
www.thewildrosepress.com